THE SURVIVALIST SAGA CONTINUES

Well readers, the world is certainly not becoming a better place. Death reaches out and strikes without reason or plan because that it is the way of life, the living must learn to deal with it. Hearts may be broken but the human spirit strives to fight back and continue on. Otherwise there is no hope, no hope for a better day, a better tomorrow.

Michael thought he could bring about a better future when he became the President of the United States, so far his job has brought the Rourkes nothing but grief. He must do something to stop this downward spiral of corruption and power struggles, organizations determined to destroy the world and re-build it to their evil specifications. Unholy alliances are forming even as we speak. Even those thought to have died centuries ago have come to bring about the downfall of the human race. What if he has a plan? Can it be implemented in time? Who can he trust?

Paul has stepped up his role in protecting his loved ones but always wonders if he's doing what his mentor, John Thomas Rourke, would do. Is he doing enough? The skills he learned on the trail riding across America so many centuries ago come into play as he must strike out on a new quest, one that could mean life if he succeeds or death for the family if he doesn't.

A posse is forming, known to only a select few. Their goal is simple—SAVE MANKIND!

Sharon

Books in The Survivalist Series by Jerry Ahern

#1: Total War
#2: The Nightmare Begins
#3: The Quest
#4: The Doomsayer
#5: The Web
#6: The Savage Horde
#7: The Prophet
#8: The End is Coming
#9: Earth Fire
#10: The Awakening
#11: The Reprisal
#12: The Rebellion
#13: Pursuit
#14: The Terror
#15: Overlord

Mid-Wake
#16: The Arsenal
#17: The Ordeal
#18: The Struggle
#19: Final Rain
#20: Firestorm
#21: To End All War
The Legend
#22: Brutal Conquest
#23: Call To Battle
#24: Blood Assassins
#25: War Mountain
#26: Countdown
#27: Death Watch

Books in The Survivalist series by
Jerry Ahern, Sharon Ahern and Bob Anderson
#30: The Inheritors of Earth
#31: Earth Shine
#32: The Quisling Covenant
#33: Deep Star

The Shades of Love (Short Story)
Once Upon a Time (Short Story)
Light Dreams (Short Story)

The Rourke Chronicles by
Jerry Ahern, Sharon Ahern and Bob Anderson
#1 Everyman

Books by Sean Ellis
Camp Zero
(*Camp Zero* series is based on characters created by Jerry Ahern, Sharon
Ahern and Bob Anderson in *The Survivalist* series.)

Coming Soon
Ice Fall, Book II in the *Camp Zero* series

THE SURVIVALIST

#34

LODESTAR

SPEAKING VOLUMES, LLC
NAPLES, FLORIDA
2016

THE SURVIVALIST
#34 LODESTAR

ISBN 978-1-62815-537-2

THE SURVIVALIST

#34

LODESTAR

Jerry Ahern
Sharon Ahern
Bob Anderson

To our readers, some of whom are featured in this episode, who were winners in a contest that Sharon Ahern initiated late in 2015. They are fans and friends of the Rourke family and now have "joined in" the adventure themselves. Welcome aboard and remember to Plan Ahead. Watch the news at www.jerryahern.com for word of another possible contest.

We also want to thank Mr. Kirk Hansen and the owners and staff at Fantastic Caverns in Springfield, MO, for allowing us access to the Caverns for the Rourke family in this growing period of unrest.

"The only person who ever truly has their revenge is the person who has nothing to lose but that chance at making something right, the person willing to crawl through the flames of hell to achieve that goal, the person who digs far more than two graves, the person overrules the judge, surpasses the jury and becomes the executioner. They are the vengeance..."

–Joshua R. A. Moore

Lodestar—Something or someone that leads or guides a person or group of people.

> 1. *archaic*: a star that leads or guides; *especially the North Star*

> 2. one that serves as an inspiration, model, or guide

First known use the 14th century, Middle English *lode sterre,* from *lode* course, from Old English *lād* (Source: Merriam/Webster Dictionary).

Prologue

Of all of the Rourke/Rubenstein children, Paula had often felt both the most responsibility and resentment. Caught on the cusp of having to 'watch out' for the others and be a kid herself often weighed on her. Now, the adventure of the John Thomas Rourke Survival Academy was thrusting her, her cousins and brother into difficult training—things that could be real life or death scenarios.

She was both excited and yet... not a little bit resentful. *Would I have to be doing this if I wasn't a Rourke?* she wondered. *Why can't I just have a normal life, like my friends?* For the first time, she seriously had to think what being a Rourke was costing her. *Is it worth it?* she wondered, right along with, *what choice do I have?*

She was about to say the world wasn't a crazy place anymore when she acknowledged the reason she and the others were on the plane. Her step-father, Wolfgang Mann, the President of New Germany, had been assassinated in a rocket attack that had leveled the German Presidential residence in New Brandenburg. A few weeks before, her Uncle Paul had been taken hostage briefly by agents of the Russian government.

Her half-brother Michael, who just happened to be President of the United States of America, had barely survived an assassination attempt and had spent several weeks in hiding. Her dad, John Rourke, was long overdue in returning from a secret assignment somewhere, and although her mother wouldn't admit anything, Paula knew he was in trouble. And now little Eddie, her baby brother was dead due to a terrible plague.

Okay, so the world really is still a crazy place.

*****

The creature known as The Creator looked at Rourke. We... are... not... so... different... from... you. The... differences... are... small... in... comparison... to... our... similarities.

"But," John Rourke's mind was spinning now. "How is that possible?"

It... is... simple. We... were... created... as... your... species... was. The... same... way. We... and... all... sentient... life... forms. More... similar... than... different.

Rourke thought a moment. "Our species is thought by some to have evolved. Others believe we were created by God. Are you familiar with that concept?"

God... yes... that... is... accurate.

Chapter One

The ICU waiting room was silent. Finally, Paul stood and said, "All right, there is nothing more we can do here. Natalia, would you take Emma and Sarah home? Tim, I think it would be a good idea if you stayed with them tonight. Annie, you and I need to start working on the arrangements in the morning, and morning is coming in just a few hours."

Croenberg stood. "How may I be of assistance, Paul?"

Paul thought for a moment. "Otto, I think the first thing is to get everyone home and rested. Would you follow them to make sure that Sarah and Emma get home safely and Tim is settled there with them? Natalia, have the Secret Service detail check in with me when all of that is done and you're home safely also." Natalia nodded her assent. "Otto, could you help me and Annie in the morning coordinate the arrangements?"

"Would 9:00 A.M. be early enough to arrive?" Croenberg asked. When Paul nodded, Croenberg escorted the others to their vehicles and waved good-bye to Paul.

*****

Michael Rourke stared out the side window of the aircraft that was returning him to the capital. Returning empty handed, the attempt to rescue his father… a dismal disappointment. The giant underwater Russian facility, thought to be where John Rourke was being held… wasn't. The glimmer of hope for John's return dashed into nothingness. Deep Star held nothing… except the bodies of Russians trapped there since before The Night of the War. Bodies that had disintegrated into dust when disturbed.

The copilot tapped him on the shoulder. "Mr. President… I am afraid I have more bad news for you, Sir." He handed Michael a note. Michael stared at it, reading it three times before the message sunk in. More bad news. Little Eddie, his young half-brother, baby Eddie… had been claimed by the deadly Hantavirus plague being spread by the genetically modified bugs. The loss of his father and now the baby crept through the dark recesses of his soul, surmounted only by the feelings of helplessness and... his own incompetence. Another failure.

Chapter Two

The next day Paul heard Emma and Sarah lamenting, "If only we had sought medical attention sooner... If only we got a second opinion from another doctor..." *If only,* Paul thought. *If only the world was a better, safer place. If only God had smiled on little Eddie. If only...* There were no words...

Tim Shaw had sent an emergency message. Michael was returning from the operation that should have rescued John... but did not. The children were at the Survival Academy. Natalia and Annie had rallied to support Emma and Sarah who felt such guilt because they had not been able to do more. Tim Shaw, normally pragmatic and in control, was devastated. Paul knew it was up to him now to be that constant never moving point of reference. He had been that for Annie and their children. Now he had to do it for the entire family. *No one can fill John Rourke's boots,* he thought. *But I have to try.*

Moments ago, Annie crawled into bed and cried softly before finally drifting off into a troubled sleep. Paul waited a few moments to be sure Annie was resting and got up, walked to his study and closed the door. Paul Rubenstein sat alone, his mood as dark as the night sky outside; alone for the first time since Eddie's death. What had happened, and its pain, had finally become reality.

This was a new position for him. Since that first time he had met John Thomas Rourke, Rourke had been "the guide," the constant, the never moving point of reference—like Polaris, the North Star, the lodestar. Paul had navigated successfully through the unsettled waters of life because of that constant point of reference. Now... now that lodestar was gone; maybe forever.

Now he was madder than hell. He would use that anger as John Rourke had taught him to. He began to formulate a plan, hopefully a plan that would keep the insanity of his situation from overwhelming him again.

What had John said so long ago? Then the words came back to him. "When faced with certain destruction from which there is no escape, no way out... Do something even if it is wrong. Just by acting you begin to change those circumstances. Simplify the complex, reduce it to its most basic level and go back to basics. It is the same problem, what you change is how you look at that problem; that changes everything."

Paul pulled a note pad from the corner of his desk and started a list. The mere physical action calmed him; at least this was something that he could do. The last stage of grief is acceptance; Paul had enough loss in his life to know that grief comes back again and again. Accepting the fact of loss never truly occurs. Accepting a challenge that could prevent that loss from possibly occurring again... that's what Paul realized he had to focus on.

The funeral would be the next act in this somber play; Eddie would be laid to rest. The family would forever be changed. Softly he murmured, "God, give me the strength to lessen the blow for my family." When Paul finally closed the notepad, his list was VERY long. Silently he crawled back into bed with Annie and closed his eyes.

Sleep came but it was not peaceful, not in the least.

Chapter Three

Peter Vale smiled; the plan had had an unintended impact. John Rourke's infant son had died as a result of the plague. He dialed Phillip Greene's private number.

"Hello."

"It is time we meet again, Mr. Greene," Vale said.

*****

The funky, dark green pickup truck was still dirty and dented and dark smoke continued to bulge from the exhaust pipe. Greene chugged down Diamond Head Road, past the old volcano and continued straight on Kahala Avenue. He knew the route by heart; he and Vale had met here many times, each time Greene felt an intense anxiousness prior to the meetings. Many times that anxiousness continued on in his heart even when the meetings had ended.

After several switchback turns and false leads as to his direction, Greene drove up the hill and parked off to the side of the road and walked half a block back down Pupukea Road. After several minutes spent making sure he was not followed, he walked back to the truck and drove about a mile to the end of the road and parked. As he walked down the red dirt trail toward the ocean, he could feel Vale's presence in the darkness surrounding him.

"It is a lovely night, isn't it, Mr. Greene?"

Greene turned as Vale stepped out of the shadows. "Yeah, I guess so."

"Oh, Mr. Greene... Look around you, moonlight riding on the waves, stars glistening in the night sky. Truly beautiful."

"If you say so."

Vale chuckled, "Mr. Greene, you are way too tense. Our plan is progressing nicely, even better than I expected."

"If you say so."

Vale turned slowly and looked at Greene. "The attack on Bellevue resulted in Wolfgang Mann's death and virtually wiped out the government of New

Germany, with zero losses on our side. John Rourke is still missing and presumed dead. His infant son has died from the plague spread by our mutant insects. The governments around the world are now seeing we can strike anywhere and at anytime. The U.S. government, under Michael Rourke's leadership, is chasing its tail trying to get ahead of something they can't even see; stumbling over themselves in the process."

"If you say so."

Vale's gaze grew cold. "Mr. Greene, if you are unable to appreciate all that is being done for your benefit… I must conclude you are either so myopic you can't see the overall picture or you are too fearful of the potential future to be an effective partner. Will it be necessary for me to look elsewhere? Tell me now. I do not have time to waste."

Sweat broke out on Greene's upper lip. He fumbled in his pocket to remove a handkerchief and dabbed the drool from the corner of his mouth. The nerve damage resulting from his last confrontation with Michael Rourke had not healed yet.

"No, that will not be necessary, Mr. Vale," he finally said. Taking a deep breath he continued, "You misinterpret my caution… I appreciate what you are doing and I do see the overall picture. Fearful? No, I'm not fearful. I simply am struggling to understand what you want of me right now."

Vale smiled. "What do I want of you? That is simple Mr. Greene. I want you to be ready. I want you ready to move to the next level of the plan." Grinning he continued, "You have heard the adage, 'to make an omelet you must first break some eggs?' I have started breaking the eggs… are you ready to mix the ingredients together?"

"Yes… yes I am," Greene said. "I only want you to direct the sequence for me. You have the operational end of this plan; the attack on New Germany was brilliant. But I knew nothing of it ahead of time; it caught me flat footed."

"As it should have, Mr. Greene. It is imperative that your responses appear genuine. After all, I am constructing the end of the world as we know it. And…" Vale said slowly, "I'm positioning you to pick up the pieces and put them all back together again."

"Back together again?" Greene asked. "Back together but different, correct?"

"Correct. You will gain the glory as the savior of your country. And in the process, you will be able to eliminate all of your enemies, all of your opposition and all of your potential problems."

Greene dabbed the corner of his mouth again with the handkerchief. "Then I turn the country over to you and your people?"

Vale laughed. "Of course not, Mr. Greene. You will soon be the President of the United States. To the world you will lead the country out of the devastation I am generating." Vale's smile vanished and his voice grew cold. "You will lead the country, I promise. But you will lead it in the directions I dictate. You will go through the steps I dictate, exactly in that order and at the times I dictate."

"And for doing that?"

"For doing that... and only that... your ambitions will be realized and you will live a life of wealth and privilege." Vale smiled and thought, *However, that life of wealth and privilege will be short lived. I will replace you with one of my men. You fool!*

Chapter Four

The drone of the plane's engines had put everyone but Paula Rourke to sleep. The news of the assassination of her step-father, Wolfgang Mann, had shocked all of the Rourke/Rubenstein children. Of all of the children, Paula often felt both the most responsibility and resentment. Caught on the cusp of having to 'watch out' for the others and be a kid herself often weighed on her.

The training at the John Thomas Rourke Survival Academy was hard. She thought, *Yeah, great training for things that could be real life or death scenarios. Sure, I am a little bit excited by it, but I'm also more than a little bit resentful. Would I have to be doing this if I wasn't a Rourke,* she wondered. *Why can't I just have a normal life, like my friends?*

For the first time, she seriously had to think what being a Rourke was costing her. *Is it worth it?* she wondered, right along with, *what choice do I have?* She frowned. *I was about to say the world wasn't a crazy place any more. A few weeks ago, Uncle Paul was taken hostage briefly by agents of the Russian government.*

Michael, who just happens to be President of the United States of America, had barely survived an assassination attempt and spent several weeks in hiding. My dad is long overdue from a secret assignment somewhere, and although Mother wouldn't admit anything, I know he is in trouble. And now little Eddie; dead from that terrible plague.

Okay, so the world really is still a crazy place.

She studied her cousins and her brother as they slept. *Their faces are so peaceful. Was that the way Michael and Annie used to sleep before their world ended?* She shook herself loose from those feelings and those questions. *After all, for better or worse I am a Rourke. So I have to make it for 'better,'* she decided.

An hour later, the plane began its descent. *Won't be long now,* Paula thought. Thirty minutes passed before they disembarked from the plane. Paula and Tim led the way, Paula holding Sarah Ann's hand. John Michael and Natalie followed a little slower. John Paul was the last off the plane; he stood on the ramp looking out across the tarmac.

"Are you guys alright?" Paul asked as he hugged Natalie and Jack.

"Yes, just glad to be home Daddy," Natalie said. "Even under these circumstances." Jack just nodded and smiled. Paul loaded the kids up in the van while the Secret Service vehicles received the luggage.

*****

For the next fifty-two hours, time crawled by at a snail's pace.

The small convoy pulled away from the curb. A Secret Service vehicle escorted the three family vehicles through the downtown traffic to the cathedral; another Secret Service car trailed behind. Four other vehicles paralleled the route on side streets ready to converge on any threat reported over the secure channel radios mounted under each dashboard. The nine vehicles moved toward the church.

Each agent dreaded the second location—the cemetery. It was too open, too hard to control, too many chances for something to go absolutely to crap. Gloomy, heavy overcast clouds blocked the sun, and the wind had a chill to it.

Michael and Natalia had Sarah with them, John Paul had insisted on riding with Paul and Annie and the rest of the children. Tim Shaw drove Emma and Emma's oldest, Paula. The mood in all of the vehicles was as dark as the sky. When the motorcade stopped, Michael and Natalia helped Sarah from the vehicle and started inside. Sarah stopped, looked at the sky and frowned.

Paula had her arms around Emma and was quickly joined by Tim, John Paul and Jack. They formed a protective circle around Emma; their faces were set and jaws locked. Natalie held Sarah Ann's hand as Paul and Annie followed the others.

Paul looked at the skies and said softly, "Not good weather for a funeral, God. Would you work up a little sunshine, please?" Annie squeezed his arm. Waiting on the steps was a tall, slender man. Beneath the disguise, Paul recognized Otto Croenberg.

9

As Michael approached, Croenberg removed his hat and spoke. "Michael, it would be my honor to assist you and the ladies. With your permission..." Michael nodded. Otto extended his arm to Sarah, she took it. Turning to Emma he said, "Mrs. Rourke you have my deepest sympathies on your loss." Emma said nothing, just giving a slight nod of her head.

Once inside, an usher guided the family to their designated seats. Tim Shaw and his son Eddie were already waiting. Tim took Emma's arm and guided her to her seat; Eddie sat beside Paula. Michael stood until everyone else was seated and walked to the front and spoke with the minister for a moment and returned to his seat. Croenberg moved to the wall next to them and stood unobtrusively, watching.

Croenberg still wore his overcoat and kept both hands in his pockets. Periodically, he shifted his weight from foot to foot. His left hand was slid through a slit in his pocket and held a 9mm assault pistol patterned after the Russian Scorpion. That left his right arm free for Sarah or to shake hands; he was an excellent shot with either hand. He also wore one of the Secret Service ear pieces and a throat microphone concealed by his tie.

Paul Rubenstein also wore a flesh colored ear wig receiver in his right ear. He was focused on the family and the funeral. He knew that Croenberg was focused merely on the family. Croenberg would disrupt a meeting of Congress to protect Sarah Rourke-Mann.

Chapter Five

The minister walked to the podium and the service began as Paul sat, staring. His jaw line was set, hard with bulging, ridged muscles. His body tense with anger. As he watched the others, his heart heaved with loss. He silently spoke to God, *I'm sorry God, right now I have a problem with praising You while I'm so very angry that such a thing has happened to a baby. Why does something started by adults have to claim the lives of children?*

Classifying himself as a "semi-practicing Jewish man married to a Gentile," it took him a while to recall the Jewish Mourner's Kaddish. It had been many years since he had last said them. In a whisper, he barely heard himself as he said them now, "Glorified and sanctified be God's great name throughout the world which He has created according to His will. May He establish His kingdom in your lifetime and during your days, and within the life of the entire House of Israel, speedily and soon; and say, Amen.

"May His great name be blessed forever and to all eternity. Blessed and praised, glorified and exalted, extolled and honored, adored and lauded be the name of the Holy One, blessed be He, beyond all the blessings and hymns, praises and consolations that are ever spoken in the world; and say, Amen.

"May there be abundant peace from heaven, and life, for us and for all Israel; and say, Amen. He who creates peace in His celestial heights, may He create peace for us and for all Israel; and say, Amen."

He felt Annie squeeze his hand and turned to look at her; tears ran down her cheeks. He turned to look at Emma. She sat to the right of her father, Tim Shaw, his arms wrapped around his daughter. *She looks like hell, but who wouldn't at a time like this,* Paul thought. Her brother, Detective First Grade Eddie Shaw, sitting on Emma's right, turned and looked into Paul's eyes then slowly turned back.

The cathedral seating was laid out in almost a semicircle and he could see Michael, Natasha and Sarah Rourke-Mann to Emma's left. *Sarah looks as drained as Emma,* he thought. All of the Rourke and Rubenstein children sat on the pews behind their parents. The girls sniffled and cried silently and the boys sat with eyes locked forward as stoic as they could be at their ages. Michael and Natalia's oldest, John Paul, would officially be a teenager in three weeks. He had his arm around his sister, Sarah Ann; tomorrow was her tenth birthday. *Not going to be much of a party,* Paul thought.

Natalie and her brother, John Michael, sat behind him, each resting a hand on Annie's shoulder. John and Emma's oldest, Paula, was holding hands with her brother, Tim, and daubing her eyes with a tissue. Paul removed his wire framed glasses and looked up at the domed ceiling. *Where are you John? You should be here.* No answer came to him.

Finally, mercifully, it was over. Paul could not tell how long it had lasted, but it felt like years. *The coffin… it's so little,* he thought. When they walked outside, Paul stopped and stared. The skies were clear, the sun brilliant, and the breeze gentle and warming. He looked higher into the heavens and said softly, "Thanks, I appreciate it."

It took thirty minutes to drive to the cemetery, twenty minutes more for everyone to get into position. Twenty minutes later, the graveside service was complete and people began to drift back to their cars… back to their lives. Most stopped and offered their condolences. Soon there was just the family left. Croenberg hovered in the background, protectively and vigilant but silent. Michael and Tim guided Sarah and Emma back to the cars along with Natalia and the girls.

Paul turned to Annie. "Go ahead, ride with them. I'll see you at Emma's when everything here is finished." She nodded and followed the others.

The girls had ridden back with Michael and Natalia. Paul, Tim and Eddie Shaw, Otto and the boys waited until the coffin was lowered and the grave filled in. It hadn't been coordinated or planned that way; it was just the way it happened. Then it was all finished.

Paul shook hands with each of them. Eddie, John Paul and Tim left with Tim Shaw. Paul put his arm around Jack and followed by Croenberg, walked back toward his car. Paul stopped and went back to the gravesite, alone. He knelt down and spoke softly. "John, it is over. I did the best I could, I hope you are pleased. If you are where Eddie is now, be at peace. If not, when you come home, I'll bring you here."

He rose, walked back and put his arm around Jack's shoulder.

Through it all, Otto Croenberg remained silent and on guard. He was somewhat surprised to feel the intensity of feelings where Rubenstein was concerned. He finally shrugged off the feelings and decided he truly did care for the Jew—and Sarah.

Chapter Six

FBI Special Agent Hiram Ellis sat outside Tim Shaw's office, waiting for Shaw to call him in. He had been waiting almost an hour when the door to Shaw's office opened and Shaw waved him in. "Sorry about the wait Ellis, things are moving pretty quickly and not always in a straight line."

Ellis smiled. "Never like waiting Mr. Shaw, but I understand. You saw my report I take it," taking a proffered cup of coffee from Shaw.

"Yeah, that's why I wanted to see you. We have confirmed John Rourke's attempted kidnapper's story, Arin Ágústsson. I spoke to the Detective Chief Superintendent of Iceland's National Police myself."

Ellis smiled again. "I take it you haven't figured out how to pronounce Yfirlögregluþjónn?" and sat down across from Shaw.

Shaw smiled. "Hell no and how did you?"

"Arin spent some time with me on it."

Shaw looked up. "Arin, huh?"

Ellis blushed a little. "You have to admit, she is a looker."

"No argument there." Shaw leaned back. "Agent Ellis, the Superintendent filled in some blanks for me and it ties into an investigation we are doing. Have you ever heard of someone called Peter Vale?"

Ellis thought for a moment and frowned. "The name is vaguely familiar but I can't... wait a minute. I saw his name tied to something about the Neo-Nazi movement."

Shaw nodded. "Correct, and we think he is choreographing an operation here against the President and his family. It appears he is tied to the assassination of New Germany's President, Wolfgang Mann, as well. Any idea where he is right now?"

Ellis shook his head. "No, no I don't. How reliable is your information?"

"His name has come up before, but this was straight from the Superintendent. Anyone in your section working on Vale?"

"Not in mine, but could be someone in one of the other sections. Have you asked the Director?"

"No, that was my next step. Thought I would start with you."

Chapter Seven

The house seemed still. The kids had gone to bed and this was the first time in days they were truly alone. Paul sat on the bed, waiting on her. Annie came out of the shower barefoot with a fluffy terry cloth robe covering her body as she vigorously dried her hair with a towel. Paul sat watching; she really was beautiful, he decided. She put down the towel and started brushing her hair. He patted the bed next to him. "Come here a minute, Sweetheart."

She smiled and sat down, still brushing her hair.

"Annie, I have some questions for you; something I'd like you to think about before answering."

"What?"

"I want to know your thoughts and memories about the time you and Michael were awake at the Retreat before the rest of us woke up. What did you like about it? What did you not like about it? How could it have been made better?"

Annie stopped brushing her hair and was silent for a long moment, going back in time… into her memories. "Here are my first thoughts. I had conflicting feelings about the Retreat. On one hand, I liked the fact that we had it. Without the Retreat none of us would have survived. But, at the same time, I hated the fact that it was necessary. I was just a little girl and did not understand what was happening or why. Does that make sense?"

"Yes."

"When Daddy first woke me and Michael up, I thought it was over… we had made it. But it was just starting. He trained us, taught us what we would need to know. That part was hard work but, for a while, I had so much time with him. That was new for me. Except for Michael, I had him almost to myself." She paused. "I think that was when I really got to know him, to… understand him. How he thought, why he was the way he was.

"He knew by doing it this way, we would have a better chance of survival as adults. He taught us all he could about preserving and maintaining the Retreat. He taught us plumbing, electrical repair and what to do if a problem arose with the cryogenic chambers as well. He gave us medical knowledge way beyond first aid, survival skills that would be necessary if we were outside the Retreat for any prolonged period of time and anything and everything else he could possibly think of that would be necessary.

"We learned to read the stars so we could navigate at night and know when to plant crops outside that would survive in the now, much shorter growing seasons. We both learned how to cook well balanced meals from the foods that we grew both inside and outside the Retreat, and how to preserve and stockpile what we didn't need for immediate use, for those leaner times. We learned to shoot and maintain every firearm in the Retreat's arsenal."

Her eyes glistened as she recalled more memories, saying with enthusiasm, "We repaired our clothes and even fabricated new outfits! He taught us it was more important to know how to find the answers than it was to know everything. Knowledge was a never ending process; one bit of information would lead to another of equal or greater importance and then another.

"The most essential skill he tried to teach us was to be able to solve problems based on accurate information and logic. He also taught us that when not enough information was put forward and logic didn't seem to matter, it might be necessary to think outside of the box. We knew if there was an emergency, some impending disaster, we could wake him up and he would attempt to solve the dilemma, but we were to use that option only as a last resort. We never had to."

She paused and said thoughtfully, "He had thought of everything, or at least that was the way I felt." She frowned. "How could it have been made better? I remember when we first went into it, how big it seemed. But after a while... it began to seem so small, I remember. When we started exploring outside the Retreat, the sun felt so good, the colors were incredible. I heard sounds I had not heard in so long. After he went back into cryogenic sleep, Michael and I explored outside the Retreat for the first time by ourselves."

She stopped and looked at Paul. "This isn't just curiosity, is it?"

"No."

She nodded. "I remember thinking about you during that time, before I was a woman and in love with you. You made me smile when I was a little girl. I'll never forget Michael and me playing poker with you before we went into the cryogenic sleep and you let us win every hand. Michael told Momma that you owed him thirteen trillion dollars!" Paul smiled, remembering. He took Annie's hand into his as she continued remembering.

"I would walk past your chamber and look at your sleeping face and wonder what it would be like when I could talk to you and tell you all the things that I'd learned about all these years. I wanted to learn more about you, too. Things besides the fact you weren't a very good poker player. I didn't think you were cheating to let us win, but I was just a little girl.

"I remember the first time I wondered... wondered, would you care that I had only been a little girl when we met. Would you only know me as the little girl hanging onto her mother or running around giggling? Wouldn't you rather hang out with the grownups, the real grownups that grew up and lived in the same outside world as you had?

"I remember once when a flash of light bolted across the back of the room, highlighted in the shadows and disappeared in an instant later. It scared me. I wanted Michael to be home, back with me. I made myself concentrate, I thought about what Daddy would say, 'Annie, stand up to your fears and go after them, don't let them come after you. Always be able to seize control of the situation and don't let go.'"

She paused and looked deeply into Paul's eyes. "Taking a deep, cleansing breath, I walked forward, heading towards the far end of the greenhouse where I thought I saw another flash of light skitter across the cold, hard, granite floor.

"I felt something I had never felt before... I felt you. I heard you in my mind but I didn't realize it was you or what was happening. I wasn't even sure if I heard it. *Fear. Hurt. Everything is out of control. I can't do this. I can barely breathe. Oh My God! I can't give up now. I promised I'd come back to you. A promise is a prom. . . Annie. Hear me, please.*"

Letting go of Paul's hand, she quickly stood up. "I remember a sudden pain gripped my chest just as a bright light flashed right in front of my face. I dropped a jar of strawberry jam and it broke on the floor. Pain hit me again and I think I passed out. Michael found me; he picked me up and put me on the couch.

"He said when I started to wake up, I said something like, 'I can't move or even open my eyes but I know you can hear me. Something's wrong, hard to breath, hard to think. Maybe I'm dying. Maybe I am dead and it's too late; too late to ever see you again, my pretty little girl. Too late to hear your laugh again. Something's wrong. Can you help?'

"Michael realized something was very wrong and went to check the cryogenics chambers. He said I had followed him and, still in that strange voice, I was saying, 'I wanted to live . . . to take care of you.' He thought I was talking to him but I wasn't. It was you, you were talking through me. You were dying in the chamber, it had malfunctioned. Luckily Michael was able to fix it, but if you had not contacted me... If you had not spoken through me... you would have died and we would not have known it for a long time."

She smiled at him. "I think that was the moment I realized I loved you. Not as a little girl but as the woman I would be one day." She sat back down on the bed next to him, taking his hand into hers. "That is my very best memory from that time. If you will give me a while to gather my thoughts, I could tell you more. Will that be alright?"

"Absolutely, that's what I was hoping you'd say." He smiled and hugged her tightly. "Michael has asked me to take a trip to Mid-Wake. The university has the best archives available and he needs some research done; probably only take a day or two. We can talk more when I get back."

"When are you leaving?"

"He said it is pretty important. Will you be okay with me leaving in the morning?"

She nodded. "But you have some 'husbandly duties' to take care of first." She kissed him hard on the lips then stood, walked over and lit two candles on the dresser and turned out the bedroom light. Turning she slid out of the terry cloth robe and smiled. "It has been too long without you."

Chapter Eight

The next morning, Paul left earlier than usual; he had a plane to catch. Michael and Tim Shaw were getting the children back to the airport so they could return to the Survival Academy.

None of them were really ready to go back but at the same time they were ready to escape the gloominess surrounding the rest of the family. Paula particularly had spent the time trying to ease her mother past something no mother should have to face. It hadn't worked.

Paul was off to Mid-Wake University to meet with Steven Delervello. Paul had met Delervello when he was working on the first volume of the Rourke Chronicles. His knowledge of the elements prior to The Night of the War, and after, was encyclopedic. Though not formally trained in any particular scientific discipline, he had made a life study of what had happened, what people back then thought would happen, and what really happened.

The trip to Mid-Wake was uneventful and as exciting as ever, especially plunging beneath the ocean waves and the first view of the giant underwater city that had been the cradle of civilization's rebirth for America.

Walking into the university's main building, Paul approached the receptionist. "Hi, I'm Paul Rubenstein and I have an appointment with Steven Delervello."

The female receptionist picked up the phone and punched a number on the dial. "Mr. Delervello, your appointment is in the lobby." She gave directions to Delervello's office on the third floor and pointed to the elevator.

Steven Delervello, five foot, seven inches tall with short salt and pepper hair, greeted Paul as he stepped out of the elevator. "Mr. Rubenstein, pleasure to see you again."

Paul looked perplexed. "Steve, I just realized I don't know your title; is it mister or doctor?"

Delervello chuckled. "I'm probably one of a very few on the staff here that is still just a mister."

Paul shook Delervello's hand. "You are still over the archives, correct?"

"Yes sir, my official title, somewhat grandiose for my taste, is Grand Archivist."

Paul smiled. "I believe that President Rourke told you the areas I would like to examine?"

Delervello took Paul's arm and guided him down the hallway. "He did. I have a private viewing area already set up for you and the materials are waiting for you. Everything dealing with before and after The Night of the War. I'll check in with you in a couple of hours to see how you're doing. If you need me before then, just come to the office; I'll be cleaning up some paperwork this morning. Oh, I took the liberty of having coffee set up for you."

Paul thanked him and followed Delervello into the viewing area. The Archivist showed him how to operate the viewing stations and begin searches for specific data before leaving. Paul pulled two legal tablets out of his briefcase, poured a cup of coffee and dug in.

*****

A knock came at the door. Paul looked up as Delervello stuck his head in. "How's it coming?"

Paul glanced at his watch and smiled. "Didn't realize so much time had passed. It's going well but there are a couple of questions, if you have a minute."

Delervello stepped in and sat down across from Paul. "Sure."

"I've tried to determine why the world survived after The Night of the War. Everyone back then was assured that nuclear war would wipe out the human race, but it didn't."

Delervello leaned back, balancing his chair on the back two legs. "Have you ever heard of the Chaos Theory?"

Chapter Nine

Paul shook his head. "I've heard of it but I don't understand it."

Delervello smiled. "I don't know that anyone can truly explain it. The Chaos Theory is simply a mathematical process that studies complex systems, systems containing a great number of variables or objects in motion. It attempts to explain what most folks believe is unexplainable. It is tied to Quantum Mechanics rather than determinism."

"Determinism?"

"Yes, the belief that everything is based on cause and effect. That which goes up must come down. In the Chaos Theory, what goes up... might come down or it could go anywhere. Much of what was thought in the Twentieth Century about nuclear weapons and long term disturbance of climate, residual radiation, and the long term effects of a nuclear war, simply did not hold up. Now that's not to say it was all disproved; radiation was devastating but not as devastating as it was feared. The earth was far more resilient than people thought.

"In a geologically very short period of time, earth's weather system stabilized, colder than before but stable. Somehow, animals survived both The Night of the War and the resulting cataclysm of the fire in the atmosphere."

Delervello stood and poured himself a cup of coffee, refilled Paul's and sat back down. "Following the nuclear launches, events moved pretty quickly toward the end. Yes... millions died during the attack. Millions more died due to radiation, the atmospheric conflagration and nuclear winter that followed. But the terrible long term affects such as the land would not be habitable for tens of thousands of years and some of the other fears, just didn't prove out the way they were forecasted. The earth rehabilitated itself far quicker than anyone imagined.

"Once man had been almost wiped out, the earth began to heal itself and do it rather quickly. Those species of animals and birds that survived even began to migrate again." Paul nodded as he took notes. "Mankind, however, really suffered."

Delervello continued, "Shortly after The Night of the War, the French attempts at surviving the global holocaust had failed and dismally too. They had been ill-prepared, unprepared to endure centuries beneath the ground. They emerged too soon and radiation took its toll. There were still massive hot spots on the planet, where the ground radiation was of such high level that the land was thought not to be habitable for perhaps a hundred thousand years. It is true that today, there are still some areas where ground radiation is still too high for human habitation."

"I saw a report identifying that the initial radiation is released by the explosions themselves," Paul said. "But residual radiation came later from isotopes and neutron bombardment unleashed by the blasts."

"Correct. Did you see the report on Hiroshima and Nagasaki?" Delervello asked.

Paul shuffled papers to find his notes. "Yes, here it is. They both had residual radiation but it didn't last long because both bombs had been detonated over five hundred meters above street level so as to wreak maximum destruction. While there was plenty of lethal fallout in the form of 'ashes of death' and 'black rain,' it was spread over a fairly wide area."

"Most of the radionuclides and isotopes had brief half-lives, some lasting just minutes," Delervello explained. "American scientists sweeping Hiroshima with Geiger counters a month after the explosion found a devastated city but little radioactivity. Water lilies blackened by the blast had already begun to grow again, suggesting that whatever radioactivity there had been immediately following the blast had quickly dissipated.

"The Japanese thought Hiroshima and Nagasaki would be uninhabitable for seventy or seventy-five years. Radiation deaths began a week after the bombings and peaked three or four weeks later. People began to develop hair loss, purple skin blotches, and bloody discharge from various orifices and died soon after. Radiation deaths subsided after seven or eight weeks but latent effects continued to appear for a long time."

Paul thumbed through a stack of files and pulled one. "These pre-Night of the War estimates were based on the Massive First Strike model. As it turned out, the results of the bombs were catastrophic, but not nearly as catastrophic as the burning of the atmosphere."

Delervello nodded. "In practice, in a more forgiving scenario, in places where evacuees were moved to clear areas in well shielded vehicles, things weren't that bad. If a population could count on very rapid transit out of the zone, if they could be stripped, shaved, and hosed down a few times, the chances for survival increase. Of course, you are at risk of cancer for the rest of your life."

Chapter Ten

Delervello continued, "One of the benefits after The Night of the War, the push to cure cancer was realized, though too late to do much for the survivors. Today we can cure that terrible disease."

Paul poured them both another cup of coffee. "Why didn't the stream beds, sewer junctions, ditches, and low lying areas remain highly radioactive for years?"

"Where the bombs were salted with cobalt, or iodine, they did. But a lot of contamination came from the roughly 245 nuclear power plants that we knew of, not counting any that the Chinese had and didn't declare. As near as we can tell, most of those were destroyed in the first few hours. No one can be certain, but that's what reports seem to confirm."

"Then explain the nuclear winter to me."

Delervello stood and walked to a chalk board and began drawing illustrations. "Look, debris and dirt were blasted skyward by the detonations. At six to nine miles above the Earth's surface, the absorption of sunlight further heats the smoke, lifting some or all of it into the stratosphere. The smoke persisted there for years with no rain to wash it out. Those particles blocked much of the sun's light from reaching the Earth's surface, which caused surface temperatures to drop drastically. They stayed that way for decades on end.

"How long this smoke remained and how severely this smoke affected the climate once it reached the stratosphere, was dependent on both chemical and physical removal processes. It turns out that the ignition of the Earth's atmosphere probably shortened the nuclear winter and while it was devastating, the effects were reduced from thousands and thousands of years, to a few hundred." Delervello put the chalk in its holder, rubbed his hands together and sat down.

"That event actually caused the airborne particles to burn and fall out of the atmosphere via dry deposition," Delervello continued. "Once the aerosol smoke particles were cleansed, a healing began—albeit a slow one. But it was still far faster than the models had predicted. The primary impact had been felt by the ozone layer and damage to nitrogen oxides—the majority of this had been corrected within a century.

"The nuclear winter had been the next fear after radiation. Models showed a profound and severe effect on the climate causing cold weather and reduced sunlight for years, even decades, and some models said it would take centuries to correct. That was if it could be corrected. It was forecasted there would be large amounts of the firestorm's smoke and soot in the Earth's stratosphere."

"And did that happen?" Paul asked.

"Absolutely, but nature and mankind were more unpredictable than anyone thought. When the equilibrium of any system is interrupted, chaos kicks in and it is dynamic. In other words, 'Life finds a way.' As devastating as The Night of the War was, and the geological and atmospheric upheavals were that followed, it was not a global extinction event. Mankind has been dealt death blows before and survived."

Chapter Eleven

Michael had authorized Paul to "read in" Delervello on some of the issues the Rourke family were facing. Particularly those that stemmed from the archives recovered from Mount Rushmore's Hall of Records.

Delervello was troubled. He stood and began pacing. After a long moment he said, "Okay, let's play a game, Paul. Let's say, for argument's sake, the Aliens were responsible, at least in part, for The Night of the War, because Earth's major powers did not dispose of their nuclear weapons. How does that jive with our colloquial view of Colonel Vladimir Karamatsov? We have evidence that he manipulated the Soviet Union into initiating World War III. Was there a conspiracy even then between the Aliens and a rogue faction of Karamatsov's KGB Elite Corps?

"I have suspected, due to some of his comments, that Karamatsov had several nefarious plans... For example, he once said 'but some few of my faithful I would sing their names in the pages of history.' There is some evidence related to a few survivors of his KGB Elite Corps and a plan to preserve him, and those few of his Elite Corp, for awakening."

Paul nodded. "John and I thought that was possible also."

Delervello nodded and continued, "We know Karamatsov died but we know little of those few survivors of the Elite Corps. There was a Major Nicolai Antonovitch who was promoted to Colonel and a Captain Andre Popovski who Natalia described as tall and young, even though she had known him five centuries ago."

"There was an unnamed major described as one of the survivors from before The Night of the War," Paul said. "He was one of the original men from Vladimir Karamatsov's KGB Elite Corps. I suspect this major could have been Popovski, with a promotion from captain to major. Natalia told me once that he was a decent man who tried to warn her about the depravities of Karamatsov. From reports on him, he seemed capable enough, and he could have staved off defeat for nine days after Antonovitch shut down the power grid and was killed for it."

Delervello said, "As strange and improbable as this theory might seem at first glance… remember… yourself, your wife, John Rourke, his wife, son and his wife made a similar 500 year sleep to survive the end of your world."

"Yes, we know. And some of the KGB Elite Corps did also," Paul said.

Delervello thought for a moment. "What we are not sure of is, was there a second sleep like your group took? Another 150 year jump into the future? And if so, what happened to those individuals? Is there another secret base? Did they awaken from the second sleep when your group did? Could they still be asleep waiting to be awakened? If they did awaken, are they the missing factor in this equation?"

Paul nodded, concern written on his face. "You're saying if we did… they could have."

"Exactly, and if that is true it would be a logical next step to assume they are either still aligned with the Aliens or are in fact aligned with the KI." He paused for a moment. "Hell, I suppose it is even possible they could be aligned with both groups, for some purpose we have no clue about. Minimally, I'd say there is an excellent probability that a rogue group of Russian KGB operatives have aligned with the military branch of the KI."

Chapter Twelve

John Rourke sat in the corner of the room, the silver headband on the floor next to him. He pondered the recent conversation with The Creator for the hundredth time. Discussing humans and his own Alien species, the creature had said, "The... differences... are... small... in... comparison... to... our... similarities."

Rourke still could not see that statement being accurate. "How is that possible?"

"It... is... simple. We... were... created... as... your... species... was. The... same... way. We... and... all... sentient... life... forms. More... similar... than... different."

Rourke said, "Our species is thought by some to have evolved. Others believe we were created by God. Are you familiar with that concept?"

"God... yes... that... is... accurate."

Accurate. Rourke could not help but believe there was a hope hidden in that conversation. Possibly even an imperative.

He had lost track of time but he thought he had been with The Creator for about two weeks, but he realized it might be as long as three weeks. It didn't really matter; Rourke had no way of determining a twenty-four hour clock, so he had kept track of his own wake/sleep cycle. He remembered from his medical studies that your body's master clock told a person when to sleep and when to wake and when to eat and much more. That circadian rhythm, as it is called, actually takes a little over 24 hours to cycle.

Rourke heard the almost silent whoosh of the door to his cell opening and looked up.

The creature known as The Creator entered and stopped just inside the door. Rourke, naked as the day he had been born, stood holding the headband loosely in one hand. The ritual he and The Creator had developed began. After The Creator had entered the room and stopped, Rourke would stand and nod. The Creator would nod back and point at the headband.

"Sure," Rourke said and started to put the headband on while dreading the sensation of pain it always induced. Dropping to a deep, slow breath, Rourke settled the silver band on his head... *No pain,* he thought. He smiled at The Creator. "That is much better; there was no pain this time. Did you do something to make it go away?"

Yes... it... required... an... adjustment. I... have... only.... used... the... device... to... make... contact... with... duplicates.

"Clones? Is that what you mean by duplicate?" Rourke asked, raising his left eyebrow.

Yes... what... you... would... call... clones. It... was... not... properly... set... for... the... mind... of... an...

The Creator paused to find the correct word.

It... was... not... properly... set... for... the... mind... of... an... original. I... am... sorry... it... caused... you... discomfort.

"Thank you for making the adjustment," Rourke said with a slight bow. "It is appreciated."

You... are... a... complicated... species. Many... emotions... and... feelings... I... find... confusing.

"I find I am confused by your species also," Rourke said. "Possibly our confusions are the first steps toward understanding each other."

The Creator turned his head from side to side. The gesture reminded Rourke of how a dog would turn its head trying to understand a sound that was unfamiliar. Yes... it... is... possible.

Rourke nodded and walked to the table he had awakened on. Hopping up, he plopped on his naked butt, saying, "Okay, how can we progress in our understanding of each other? After all, you are the one that sought me out."

The Creator again turned his head from side to side in what was now becoming familiar. Correct... I... did... seek... you... out. It... is... necessary... if... we... are... going... to... survive.

Rourke frowned. "What do you mean if 'we' are going to survive?"

The Creator looked at Rourke for some time. Rourke could not tell if the question perplexed The Creator or vexed him. Finally, The Creator said, By... we... I... mean... we... us... you... your... people... me... my... people.

We... must... understand... each... other... or... none... of... us... will... survive. We... are... not... so... different... from....you.

I... sense... something...new... in... you. Are... you... angry... or... sick... or... troubled?

Rourke thought for a moment and decided to try the truth. "My people rely on a rhythm. Our bodies are regulated to periods of what we call day and night. We call it a circadian rhythm and it relies heavily on sight; being able to see day light and dark. In this..." Rourke gestured to his cell. "In this, I have no way of getting outside verification of the cycling of the sun and moon. People of my species who lose their ability to see, who are totally blind and have no light perception, develop difficulty both with sleeping and staying awake."

The Creator turned his head from side to side in that quizzical gesture. Rourke continued. "I have no way of keeping track of my own sleep cycles except through my memory... and after a while, that is not sufficient to maintain my body's cyclic balance. That balance releases two hormones: melatonin and cortisol. The first is tied to sleep, and the second tells me when to wake up and when to eat. Cortisol also controls my metabolism, cardiovascular function, immune system, and appetite. When my master body clock is out of sync with the typical day-night cycle, sleep deprivation makes it difficult to focus on the tasks at hand. This sleep disorder will sap my energy, causing me to fall asleep at inopportune times, and make daily tasks a challenge. It can also cause a sense of paranoia and discomfort. That is probably what you are sensing."

The Creator nodded. I... understand... What... can... I... do... to... assist... you?

Rourke frowned and thought, *Is this a trick? What the hell, let's find out.*

Rourke slid off the table and faced The Creator straight on in his nakedness. "First of all, I would like my clothes back. My species is more comfortable if our bodies are covered. Second, I need to reestablish my circadian rhythm. Is it possible to see the sun and stars again? Thirdly..." Rourke grimaced to himself. "Thirdly, I would like to get out of this room and walk. My species requires movement, what we call exercise."

The Creature turned and exited the cell without comment. Rourke took off the silver headband and turned. *Well*, he thought, *doesn't hurt to ask.*

Chapter Thirteen

After returning home from the meeting with Delervello, Paul could not shake the sense of unease. He talked with Annie and heard some more about her memories in the Retreat. Surprisingly, her memories were more pleasant and upbeat than he thought they would be. *That could be a big help with the youngsters if this thing goes the way it is looking.*

He had met briefly with Michael, and they agreed to a follow up meeting after Michael had the opportunity to converse with his Intelligence people.

Paul decided it was time to polish up some of his shooting skills. *I fear they may be needed sooner than later*, he thought. He spent the next day at the Lancer Firing Range working through several courses of fire.

*****

Jim Downey, Lancer's head engineer, had stood silently back from the firing line and did not approach Paul until he had finished one course of fire. "Morning Mr. Rubenstein, I heard you were here. Getting a little trigger time?"

Paul smiled. "Yeah, haven't had much time to practice lately. How are you doing, Jim?"

Downey smiled. "Livin' the dream, Mr. Rubenstein. I spend all day every day trying to come up with new ideas for my first love, guns. But it is hard to improve on those two babies." Downing was pointing at Paul's Schmeisser and Browning High Power. "Those designs were incredible in the twentieth century and are still today. Hey, have you tried our new Live Fire Shoot House?"

"I didn't know it was open yet."

"Last week," Downing said with a show of pride. "Want to try it out against some of the Lancer crew, with training or simulated ammunition? Basically, it is ammo loaded with special projectiles that come out of the gun like real bullets but won't hurt you. Well," Downing smiled, "won't hurt you real bad. Kinda like Paint Ball on steroids. Simple conversion on the Browning takes less than two minutes to swap parts. Don't have anything for the Schmeisser but you can use one of our converted CAR 15s if you want."

Paul smiled. "I'd love to. You have any one loose who can join me?"

Downing smiled and walked to an intercom on the wall, pushed a button to talk and said, "Hey, anyone loose who wants to take on the great Paul Rubenstein in the Shoot House with training ammo?" Four sets of "I do!" followed almost immediately. Three men approached out of the weapon repair shop, young and obviously former military or former law enforcement. The fourth came down the stairs from the second floor. Older, not as fit, and definitely not as trim.

"Mr. Rubenstein, I'm Paul Williams. I'm Lancer's Master Gunsmith."

"Pleased to meet you, Mr. Williams. You're a little older than these guys..." Paul said with a smile.

Williams grinned. "Yeah, you could say I'm too old to fight and too slow to run, but I can still shoot pretty good!"

Chapter Fourteen

Paul returned from the shooting range later in the evening than he planned. He walked stiffly into the garage and set the bag with his Browning High Power and the MP-40 Schmeisser on the work bench. His body still hurt in several places where simulated ammo had made contact. He had held his own against the three younger shooters; he was still pretty good on the fire and maneuvering that Rourke had taught him so long ago. It was Paul Williams, the oldest guy, who had been his biggest threat, and the one responsible for most of his aches and pains at the moment.

Williams never appeared to get in a hurry; he just nailed Paul at every opportunity. Paul winged him once… that was it. Paul had finally given up and asked, "Okay, Mr. Williams, what is your secret?"

Smiling, Williams had told him, "Swing by tomorrow and I'll show you, Mr. Rubenstein."

Annie was at Emma's and with the children; the house was quiet. He spread a mat on the work bench and disassembled the High Power. Next, he broke down the Schmeisser for cleaning. Soon the smell of burnt gunpowder was replaced with the aroma of gun solvent and oil. He heard the doorbell ring, went to the front door, opened it and smiled. "Hello, Otto."

"Hello, Paul. May I come in?"

"Sure, I'm working in the garage. Would you like a glass of tea?"

Croenberg sniffed the air. "Cleaning your weapons, I presume? Yes, a glass of tea would be fine."

Paul poured a glass from a pitcher and led Croenberg into the garage. "Hmmm," Croenberg said, frowning. "I see you have both of your weapons disassembled. I must say that is not a smart idea my friend."

Paul said nothing and returned to work on the Schmeisser. "What can I do for you, Otto?"

Croenberg set down the glass. "I think there might be something I can do for you my friend. Educate you a little." He flexed his arm and the tiny See-camp .32 slid into his right hand. "Like I said, having both of your weapons disassembled is not a good idea."

Paul looked over his shoulder at the .32, then he smiled without turning. "Afraid for me because I'm unarmed? Can't defend myself?"

"Exactly, my old friend. I fear you have gotten soft and are willing to drop your guard after all of these years." Croenberg slid the tiny pistol back into position.

"You are correct," Paul said. "I realized it has been too long for me to go without regular practice. Yeah, I guess I've gotten soft. However," he said, slowly swiveling his seat, turning to face Croenberg. From his right fist protruded the heavy, ugly, blue black muzzle of a two-inch, Colt .357 Lawman. "Drop my guard? I don't think so."

Croenberg smiled, "Excellent. I apologize for questioning you."

"No need to apologize." Paul smiled, sliding the .357 back into his waistband. "A few months ago, you would have probably been right. But that was before someone tried to kidnap me… before Wolfgang died… before little Eddie died. Before the plague and before the world started going crazy again. Otto, I have come to the realization that things have changed, and I have to change back."

"Back?"

Paul nodded. "Back to the way I used to feel and think; back in the days when John and I began our journey together. After this period of peace, I think we all assumed the craziness we had survived had finally ended. It hasn't, it just took a few years off. Now, it's back and John's still missing. He trained me, now it is my job to step up and try to fill the vacuum created by his absence. But, tell me why you came."

"I have two questions," Croenberg said and cleared his throat. "First, how are the ladies? They did not look well at the funeral."

Paul picked up a paper towel and wiped his hands. "Struggling, Sarah and Emma particularly. They were with Eddie and feel they should have done something sooner that might have saved him."

"That is most unlikely from what I understand about the plague."

Paul nodded. "I agree, but right now they are stuck in those feelings. Second question?"

"Why did you call me to the hospital that night?"

Paul stood. "Honestly, at the time I did not know; seemed the right thing to do at the time."

Otto nodded. "And now?"

Paul walked the length of the garage, slowly. Croenberg couldn't tell if he was searching for the words or deciding whether or not to say them aloud. Paul finally turned around to face Otto, taking a deep breath before slowly letting it out. "I need your help."

"Whatever I can do."

Paul shook his head. "It's not that simple, Otto. This is much bigger than a simple favor... Are you my friend?"

Otto took a step back. "I am."

"No Otto... are you my FRIEND? Not a buddy... are you prepared to commit to me and my family on a deeper level than you have been to anyone else?"

Otto turned away, vigorously rubbing his face with both hands, then he turned back to face Paul. "I am not sure what you are saying, but yes. Yes, I am your friend and yes, I will support you and the family however you need me."

Paul nodded and walked to a file cabinet removed two small glasses and a bottle of Seagram's. He poured two glasses and handed one to Croenberg. "Let's drink to that, Otto. We have a lot to do and very little time to have it done. I need you to be focused and watch over Annie and Sarah; I'm going to be gone, looking for something."

Clicking Paul's glass with his own, Croenberg asked, "Are you sure what you seek exists?"

Rubenstein smiled. "I know it existed at one time because I was in it, once. I was a teenager when my father, Lieutenant Colonel David Rubenstein, was transferred from Scott Air Force Base in Illinois to Barksdale Air Force Base in northwest Louisiana. While our household goods were being shipped, we drove. We crossed into Missouri and drove to Springfield. That evening, we checked into a motel and asked directions to a nearby restaurant. The desk clerk told Dad there was a nice place just up the street, 'Easy walk about a half block on the left'. Even Mom liked the idea of stretching after being cooped up in the car all day.

"We found the restaurant and got a table; there was a small placard stuck in a wire rack that held the salt and pepper shakers and napkins. It talked about Fantastic Caverns, a show cave located in Springfield, Missouri. Fantastic Caverns was the only cave in North America to offer a completely ride-through tour in a propane powered, Jeep-drawn tram. The temperature inside the Caverns stayed about 60 degrees Fahrenheit year-round.

"I remember the placard said in the winter and fall, that it was a 'warm sixty degrees,' while in the summer and spring, it was a 'cool sixty degrees.' The place hosted over 100,000 visitors a year.

"I asked Dad if we could go there the next day, before we had to drive to Louisiana. It wasn't that I was *that* interested in caves, I just wanted to delay getting back in the car as long as possible. Dad said, 'Why not?'

"The trams drove along the path left behind by an ancient underground river and we learned the cavern was discovered by a man and his hunting dog in the mid-1800s. The man did not want the cave to be exploited by the Union or Confederate governments as a possible source of saltpeter, so he kept the cave's existence secret till after the war. Then he put an advertisement in the Springfield paper for someone to explore the cave, and it was first explored after the Civil War by some women from a local women's athletic club. They were considered the first explorers of the cave, since they carved their names into the rock as graffiti and are mentioned in an article published in a local newspaper. It was named Fantastic Caverns in the 1950s.

"It was used as a hangout for a local vigilante group for a while, a speakeasy during the Prohibition years, and hosted music concerts during the 1950s and 1960s. The shows were broadcast on local radio in the 1970s. Missouri had a bunch of caves before The Night of the War, over seven thousand. This one I believe will work for what I have planned. I just have to find it and see if it survived The Night of the War or collapsed."

Otto nodded. "What do you need to make that trip?"

Paul pulled a notebook down from a counter top. "There are two phases of this trip. First, finding the cavern, I'll just be a tag along on that. But to transport the stuff from the original Retreat, I will need a stout, four wheel drive truck with a good trailer, supplies to last several days should there be a break down, a relief driver and a scout vehicle. I'm figuring on a Harley. So, me and one or two others should be able to pull it off."

Otto nodded, "How do you expect to find the cavern, if it still exists?"

"Have to go there in person. I have studied the aerials of the area, too much has changed. The good news is the old airport is still identifiable. That's where we'll start." Paul laid out a map. "The cavern is only a few miles north, northeast of the old airport. Aerial photos show the small local roads are pretty well messed up, but the old Interstate 44 and the access road from the airport should be usable. We'll have to go cross country a few miles, maybe six or seven, I'm not sure."

Croenberg studied the map and nodded. "Who is the 'we' you refer to?"

Paul straightened up and said, "I'm figuring Akiro Kuriname's Dog Soldiers and Wes Sanderson's Special Forces."

Otto looked up. "So, I take it Michael is aware of your search?"

Paul nodded, "Yes, it is an essential part of his overall plan. I need you for something else."

"What is that?"

"While I'm gone, I need you here to cover Annie and Sarah. You will be working with Tim Shaw and the Secret Service making sure that Emma, Michael and Natalia are covered. However, Annie and Sarah are your prime considerations."

"I see," was all Croenberg said.

Chapter Fifteen

Michael and Paul walked the beach together; it had become a regular event. Michael's Secret Service detail closed off both ends of a three mile stretch, and a car with five agents paced them from the street above. It was the only place either felt safe about discussing their plans. Neither spoke for the first one hundred yards of their walk. Michael finally broke the silence.

"Paul, I appreciate your help with this."

Paul glanced at Michael and nodded. "Are you still sure this is how you want to handle it?"

Michael sighed heavily, "Yeah... yeah, I am. The political pundits are already sniffing around and rumors of an all-out assault by the Progressives have started. With Otto's and other operative's input, we know they are planning a complete political restructuring of the government. The simplest way to accomplish that is for the Rourke family to be eliminated."

"I was not aware you had other operatives plugged into this."

Michael turned toward Paul and smiled. "Like Dad always says, 'it pays to plan ahead.'"

"So, have you had time to review that list I gave you?" Paul asked.

Michael nodded. "That's why I wanted to meet with you. I have and I agree with the basic plan you laid out. I have added some things and some people to the plan though. When my father was making plans for the original Retreat, it was based on his feelings and premonitions that something was going to happen. His master plan was to protect Mom, Annie and me. This new plan is based on facts and something dad didn't have."

"What do you mean?"

Michael stopped and turned to look directly at Paul. "Dad knew a lot about how the government worked and a lot about how screwed up it could become. But even he hadn't been at the level I have since the election. There are things I know he simply did not. Resources we can count on... both material and personnel. There are physical threats and real danger coming for the entire family... not to mention the country.

"I don't want the Progressives to paint us, the Rourke family, as being un-American or anti-American because of my resignation. But that is exactly what is going to happen. They are going to say, 'It looks like Michael Rourke is walking away from everything his father and the family fought to protect, taking the easy way out, being anti-American.'"

Paul grimaced. "Michael, no one will believe that."

Michael shook his head. "Some won't but many will. Our Intel shows that there is an organized faction whose goal is to destroy America, the life of freedom, and create the One World Order. Everyone is under the threat. And we can't fight it effectively the way things are structured; we are too limited, too constrained by the very laws that protect our own society."

Paul nodded. "It is how we all survived The Night of the War. We fought brigands and cannibals and Russians and tyrants and madmen of every shape and ilk. Now we have to do it again?"

Michael nodded, "Yes, yes we do. I had to ask myself 'WWJTRD—what would John Thomas Rourke do?' While this will be the hardest thing the family has had to do in a long time... I believe Dad would bless this decision."

Paul's eyes flashed, "Not 'would,' Michael. Will. As soon as we find him and bring him home... he will bless this plan." Paul took a deep breath to calm himself. "I remember, or at least think I remember, a time when politics were civil. When both sides of the aisle were American, no matter how they differed in ideology. In those days the two primary parties were the Republicans and the Democrats. Sure, third parties or alternate parties were tried periodically but they never caught on."

Michael nodded and they started walking again. "It wasn't until civilization was 'reconstituted' after The Night of the War that the terms Representative and Progressive were assigned to political parties. That was also when the aspect of the 'political climate' and 'public opinion' became so emotionally charged. Mankind was blasted back to an emotional Stone Age during that war.

"There were some 'Great Thinkers' that emerged, but they mostly espoused the thoughts of what had been called New Age before The Night of the War. Harmony, peace, tranquility—going along to get along... that kind of stuff. Hallucinogenic drugs were treated as pharmaceuticals. It was a really strange time." Michael smiled. "So, tell me exactly how you are going to pull this off?"

Paul put his hands in his pockets, stared straight ahead said, "First of all, I have to find the location for Retreat 2. Until I have that located and we begin preliminarily staging, the move from the original Retreat is superfluous. When the Caverns are located, we have to prep them to accept the people and supplies. Third, while that is going on, I head back to Georgia and start removing those items we will need from the original Retreat. While that is going on, additional supplies that you will designate will need to be moved to the Caverns."

"Yeah," Michael said. "And all of this will need to be done secretly. If news of what you're doing gets out... it is all for naught."

Paul nodded. "Exactly. The final aspect of that secrecy is your resignation from the presidency. When that occurs everything has to have already been done, and must have everything we need before the announcement is made."

"That's what worries me, Paul. We can have the first four steps accomplished and blow everything in the final one. We have to keep the Cavern location secret, once we find it. We can have transport of materials done covertly but what about the stuff you are bringing from the original Retreat.

Paul nodded. "That is going to have to be done in the open and the only cloaking capability we have is with the counter-illuminated camouflage technology recovered during the raid on the abandoned Waiāhole Ditch and Tunnel System when we found the egg-shaped UFO General Thorne has mastered. That will mean once we find the Caverns we can position those camouflage generators around it to allow us to work and prep them. That will free up Thorne's UFO to cover me on the ground trip from Georgia. The supplies you funnel to the Caverns will be the most extensive. We have to have sufficient supplies for all of the people we expect to house there, plus gear to maintain surveillance and communications until we can rejoin society. We have no idea how long that is going to take."

"Don't forget ground transportation, weapons, munitions and all of that," Michael said.

"I'm not. Here's the point Michael… the original Retreat was designed for four people to survive the end of the world and restart humanity. The reality is it functioned and succeeded but not everyone was destroyed in The Night of the War and the conflagration that followed. Had in fact everyone else been destroyed… John's plan to save his family would have only prolonged the evitable. My thought is we have to have resources and materials to support a hidden force of at least seventy-five or eighty people."

Michael shook his head. "Let's look at one hundred, twenty-five just for planning sake. And supplies… food, fuel, medical, transport… all of it—for at least five years; longer if we can do it. But remember, we still have satellite surveillance that our enemies will have access to and we can't do anything about it."

Paul smiled. "Yes, that's why we'll need Thorne and his ship and why we have to carefully pick those individuals we know we can trust. And remember what your Dad used to say, 'I'd rather go in short than stupid.' The good news is we have control of two items that are totally unique: the UFO and the camouflage generators.

"There are twelve of the counter-illuminated camouflage generators, each with the ability to create an invisibility cloak or force field that covers over seventy-odd square yards by assuming the colors and textures of that generator's surroundings. Linked together, this creates a cloaked area of about three hundred square yards. The UFO can travel, create a cloaking field, and the tractor beam can be extremely useful. We simply have to steal it… and the pilot, by the way."

"Or…" Michael said, smiling. "Or, we get the pilot and craft on our side from the beginning and rather than steal them… we enlist them. Paul, you have permission to find the Caverns. I'll contact Sullivan; he'll begin working on this and provide whatever you need."

Chapter Sixteen

Michael and General Sullivan, the Air Force Chief of Staff, sat in Michael's office. "General, here are the threats we can identify. One Peter Vale, is tied to the Democratic Republic of New Germany in Europe and I believe he is linked to our own Progressive Party. He is an international spy and provocateur, head of what is known as the Militia. It is a paramilitary force created ten years ago by the German government. It participates in summary executions and assassinations and is now expanding its influence.

"Two, Neo-Nazis to include those in South America that launched the attack on Bellevue and killed Wolfgang Mann. They employ both full and part timers as well as a youth wing. Early Neo-Nazi volunteers included members of Germany's far-right parties, such as the Action Brigade, and working-class men convinced of the benefits of Nationalist alliance. We have information they are coming here.

"Three, a bio-weapon in the form of a genetically engineered insect spreading a more deadly form of the Hantavirus.

"Four, a perceived alliance between members of the KI and what is possibly a rogue faction of the Russians.

"Five, the Alien presence we now have proof of, but no idea what they want or what they are willing to do to get it."

Michael stood and walked to the window; turning he said, "Here are the resources we can identify: One, we have an ally in The Keeper that can help root out the rogue KI and identify the Russians.

"Two, we have good intelligence to continue to track developments in the Neo-Nazi movement.

"Three, we have launched the first phase of the extermination plan dealing with the bio hazard.

"Four, we have a captured Alien craft and now know how to fly it.

"Five, it is possible, even probable, that my father has been captured by the Aliens and if that is the case… and if he is still alive… may be able to help us. At least help us to define the actual threats and refine our responses."

Sullivan said, "We are no closer than before to finding your father, Mr. President. However, we may have just found a lead. You know we have been monitoring magnetic anomalies in the Arctic region."

"Yes, have you found something?"

"Maybe, it looks promising. Of course, it could be a hoax. We received a report of what appears to be an electrical generation device powerful enough to power the continental U.S. Supposedly, it was discovered by some geologists and other scientists. It appears to be of an underground pyramid larger than the Great Pyramid of Cheops. The discovery was made by scientists who set up a whole bunch of equipment and used the seismic information to 'map' a certain area in Alaska."

"Why haven't I heard about this before?" Michael said with a frown.

"Apparently this was a discovery by a bunch of Trilateral Alliance scientists that kept it secret until they had more data. Looking to cash in on some big scientific honor or award, it appears. One of the American scientists came to me with the story. Normally, I would have blown it off, except..."

"Except for what, General?" Michael asked.

"Except for these." Sullivan handed a sheet of paper with 63°17'51.40"N, 152°31'24.49"W to the President.

"Coordinates?"

"Yes Sir, now take a look at this." Sullivan handed another sheet of paper to Michael, also with numbers and letters on it.

Michael compared the two sets of numbers. "Appear to be the same, General. Where did you get the other set of coordinates?"

"From this report, Mr. President." Sullivan slid a file across to Michael. "We recovered this from the Hall of Records at Rushmore. It is the location of an area the U.S. deeded to the Aliens in 1964; however, it appears that whatever is located there has been there much longer ago than 1964."

Michael frowned. "What is the location of these coordinates, General?"

"Near the western boundary of the Denali National Park, about 150 miles west of Talkeetna, the nearest large settlement; and some 230 miles from both Anchorage and Fairbanks and under a lot of ice and dirt. This area is located in what is called the Alaskan Bermuda Triangle."

Michael sat back in his chair. *1964,* he thought. "Am I correct that it was also the year of the Great Alaskan Earthquake?"

"You are, Sir."

"You said whatever is located there appears to have been there much earlier than 1964?"

Sullivan leaned back in his chair. "I spoke with Jose Zima, he researched it and told me there are stories from the native Alaska Tlingit and Aleut Indians that speak of evil spirits, capturing people who have drowned or were lost, whisking them away to another realm never to be seen again.

"I spoke with Steve Delervello from Archives; he said there was a report that got squashed after a 1969 Atomic test on the island of Amchitka in the Aleutian chain. They had a lot of seismological instruments set up all across Alaska to measure the shock waves from the test. They got a 'shock' alright, seems the seismological instruments painted an echo of a large underground 'something' near the National Park."

He reached over and retrieved the file from Michael, thumbing through the file until he came to a paper clipped page. He spun it around so Michael could see it and slid it back across the table.

It was a seismological chart showing a dark triangular shape with the notation. Sullivan said, "Target is approximately 100 meters below the surface, pyramidal in shape size, 830 feet per side, 481 feet high. That's roughly a 10 percent increase on the dimensions of the Great Pyramid. But, unlike the dimensions of the Great Pyramid, which have a slight variance from side to side, these are precise and exactly the same along all four sides."

"Exactly the same?" Michael queried.

"Exactly, and look at these." Sullivan walked around and pointed at the chart. "See these minor disturbances?"

"Yeah," Michael said.

"We think those could be tunnels that access the pyramid underground."

Chapter Seventeen

"You're here, Mr. Rubenstein," Paul Williams said, glancing up from his workbench. He removed the headband with magnifier lens and laid it on the bench in front of him.

"You said for me to come back and you'd tell me your secret," Paul said with a smile. "I'm here. I'm sore and I'm here and I want to know how you were able to nail me so easily yesterday."

Williams stood up, a big man over six feet tall with a full head of salt and pepper hair, though admittedly more salt than pepper. "No big secret Paul. You were jerking the trigger. It's been too long since you have been on the range. Look, combat shooting isn't like target shooting. In target shooting you take your time, you aim. You have time to think about trigger control, breath control and sight alignment. In combat, well in combat things are moving too quickly for conscious thought in most cases. You fall back on muscle memory and instinct and what and how you practiced."

"I can see that, but what are you saying I should be doing right now?"

Williams smiled. "You like grapes?"

"Do what?"

"Do you like grapes?"

"Yeah, I guess so," Rubenstein said and thought. "Yeah, I like grapes, so what?"

Williams got a big grin on his face. "Go buy some. Get about three bags. Every day for the next three days... Now this is important Mr. Rubenstein, pay attention."

"I am. Grapes, three bags... got it."

Williams continued, "Get some paper towels and go outside and put a grape between the end of your trigger finger and the knuckle where it joins your hand."

"Okay, what then? What do I do with the grape?"

Williams smiled a big, infectious smile. "You squeeze it ever so slowly. Squeeze...squeeze...squeeze until it pops. Then you eat it and wipe your hand off with the paper towel and get another and do the same thing. Do it until the whole bag is gone. Next day, same thing. Day after that, the same thing. Then come to the range and shoot, but shoot like you are squeezing the grape. You will be amazed."

*****

Four days later, Paul returned to the range and was amazed. His groups were tight, well centered. He had shot better than he ever had. He left a note of thanks on Williams' workbench, and a bag of grapes.

Chapter Eighteen

Alone in his study, Paul sat consulting old maps from before The Night of the War. He realized that it would have taken less than twelve hours to make the trip from the original retreat at Mount Yonah in Georgia to Springfield, Missouri and the Fantastic Caverns before The Night of the War.

That was when the Interstate Highways existed and there were still bridges across the Mississippi River below what had once been St. Louis, Missouri. Paul removed his wire framed glasses and closed his eyes, remembering… St. Louis.

Suddenly, he was back on the airplane… just before the Night of the War started. A woman had had a heart attack; some guy had saved her life and gone to the cabin bathroom. As he was retaking his seat, severe turbulence slammed the plane hard to the right. The man struggled to stay upright and shouted, "Everyone look away from the windows and put your heads down! Protect your faces, your eyes!" Paul thought, *I don't think I had ever been more terrified.*

That man had been John Thomas Rourke and Paul had looked down as he was instructed. Rourke had told him later that through the window he had seen something in the air. Pale white and crashing downward; a missile with a nuclear warhead. The city of St. Louis, Missouri had vanished, simply vanished in a flash of light and superheat.

Paul continued in thought, *I wondered, how many lives had been snuffed out? What were their last thoughts? Did they feel the horror of knowing what was about to happen? Did they have time to say goodbye to loved ones or was there simply a flash of blinding light followed by incineration and instant obliteration? I wonder.*

Paul rubbed his face and eyes vigorously and replaced his glasses, looking again at the maps. "Twelve hours in those days. Days, maybe weeks today," he said aloud to the otherwise empty room. Going over the satellite images, he realized that there were long stretches of four lane highway that simply did not exist any longer. Yet, strangely, the back roads appeared more or less, or at least somewhat, intact from Georgia through Tennessee and into Kentucky. On the western side of the Mississippi, the story was pretty much the same. Interstate and main highways long lost to the bombs and nature.

The New Madrid Fault line had slipped; probably at the same time the San Andreas and the unknown Floridian Fault gave way, dropping the Peninsula as well as California into the depths. It was still an active fault system which had grown from one hundred fifty miles in length to almost twice that. Extending into five states, it had swallowed Cairo, Illinois as well as Hayti, Caruthersville and New Madrid in Missouri, and all the way to Marked Tree in Arkansas.

Somehow the devastation had missed Blytheville, Arkansas, which sat directly in its path. *Maybe nature does have a sense of humor*, Paul thought. The New Madrid Fault had combined with the Wabash Valley Seismic Zone, taking parts of western Tennessee and Kentucky with it when the entire area dropped over 200 feet the instant the fault failed.

Paul studied the map, absently he said, "But it missed Blytheville..." Of course the town had been destroyed but that was a result of the earth shaking. Brick and mortar buildings never had a chance against quakes exceeding 9.0 on the Richter scale. But the satellite photos showed the contours of a ten mile section of the Mississippi River bed looked remarkably unchanged from the old maps. *That is where I am going to have to cross.*

Pushing his wire framed glasses back up off the bridge of his nose, he said aloud, "Otherwise, I have to air lift everything from the Retreat in Georgia to Springfield and that would blow any chance at keeping this a secret."

Two teams would be required to pull off the preparations necessary to ready Fantastic Caverns for its new role and the transfer of materials from the original Retreat. Rubenstein was going to do double duty with both teams. Figuring a plan for moving materials from the original Retreat to the new one, Paul recognized that he wasn't, and had never been, much of a logy or logistician.

John Rourke had always focused on that end of their "business." Of course, as their adventures had continued, Paul picked up the basics out of necessity. He and Rourke had often operated independently of each other.

John had told him once that, "In the military sense, logistics involved maintaining your own supply lines while disrupting those of an enemy. When I was stocking the Retreat, I focused on simply acquiring the right stuff, and enough of it for us. That was mostly physical items like weapons, ammo, food and other essentials. I learned very early that it took money, time and space to lay in enough 'stuff' to prepare for what I hoped would never happen."

"Money, time and space," Paul said out loud as he poured over his notes. "Well, money and space are not the great issues they were for John. Time certainly is, however." Paul knew his greatest time factor was Michael. There was a lot to do, and a lot to transport before Michael "pulled the plug" on the Presidency. Paul prayed that could be delayed a little while longer.

Otherwise... it would all have been in vain.

Chapter Nineteen

Otto Croenberg, in the persona of Darrel Johnson, was chatting with Phillip Greene in Greene's office. "I understand you will be meeting with Mr. Vale soon, is that correct?"

Greene blanched. "How... how did you know?"

"That is not relevant, Mr. Greene. What is relevant is that I had to find out about it from my own sources instead of having you advise me of it. Were I a suspicious individual, that would make me think you were going back on our arrangement." Croenberg/Johnson stood, walked to the window before turning with a malevolent smile. As he adjusted the brocade curtain he said, "That, Mr. Greene, would upset me greatly. Phillip, are you trying to upset me?"

Greene gave a nervous laugh. "Nooo, ha ha, Mr. Johnson. I would never consider going back on my deal with you."

Croenberg/Johnson affixed the radio transmitting bug to the brocade curtain with his left hand. "No, Phillip, I did not think you would. I expect a full briefing. Oh, and Phillip, I have a friend who would like to meet Mr. Vale. My friend can be of great financial assistance to his efforts. You may give him this information." Croenberg/Johnson pulled a folded piece of paper from his inside jacket pocket. "You may reach my friend at the number at the bottom of the page if Mr. Vale agrees." Greene nodded and took the paper.

*****

Croenberg sat in his car across the parking lot by Phillip Greene's office, listening to Greene and Vale discuss the future. Greene was telling Vale he had been approached with an offer of substantial financial contributions from a well-placed "Neo-Nazi" sympathizer, named Bob Yeager who wished to meet him. Croenberg knew that Vale's ego would not allow him to forego the opportunity to find out if the offer was legitimate and his greed would not let him pass up the opportunity for increased financial contributions.

Vale said, "Do you know this person?"

Greene blushed. "No I don't but I have had my staff check out this information. It seems legit. Do you want to meet with him?"

"If he passes your scrutiny, extend the invitation," Vale said. "Tomorrow morning at nine o'clock at the Saint Germaine Cafe on Alakea Street and Ala Moana Boulevard. Tell him there will be a reservation in the name of John Tomlinson, they will show him to the table. I will meet him there."

Chapter Twenty

Some part of Michael realized that he was dreaming; dreaming and re-membering. Remembering a time when he had left Annie in the Retreat and explored. The rest of the family was asleep in their cryogenic chambers. His dad had set their training in motion and returned to the sleep that had saved them all from the end of the world.

He remembered this trip, from so long ago:

He traveled for several days and was about to return to the Retreat when he saw the smoke. By the odometer on the Harley, he traveled another twenty four miles, occasionally seeing the smoke from a fire. Finally, he parked the Harley and moved out on foot. He had moved cautiously, aware that in the dry air, sound traveled long distances. The pace he had set was one that was practiced from walking the mountains near the Retreat, one he could maintain in the thinner air.

His right fist was closed on the Pachmayr gripped butt of the Stalker, his Magnum Sales converted Ruger Super Blackhawk .44 Magnum single action with 2X Leupold scope.

Threading his way through the trees, weaving back and forth, moving as soundlessly as possible, he could smell the smoke now. And he smelled something else. He didn't know what it was, but it reminded him of the last time his sister had cooked meat. But the smell was not pleasant and warming to him, it was somehow vile. His dream self was afraid, sweating as his fist tightened even more on the butt of the Stalker. He moved into a crouch… The smell…

He stood stock still as he reached the edge of the trees and could see clearly the open area beyond the clearing. The fire still smoked in the center of the clearing, blackened and smoldering. The smell was stronger as he moved into the clearing, his eyes riveted to what he saw beside the fire; a bone, white with the flesh gone. The two ends of the bone jaggedly broken.

There were more bones littering the ground near the fire. He dropped into a crouch; with the spear point tip to his big Gerber, he rolled the bone over.

The marrow from inside it had been scraped out. The bone, like the other bones littered near the fire, unmistakably human.

And so was the partially eaten, burned flesh. He fought the feeling of nausea, standing up, turning away from the fire, trying to breathe through his mouth so he wouldn't experience the smell.

Searching around, he saw it; the skull of a small child, a girl... a girl younger than Annie. The skin was gone from the top of the thing, as if scalped. Only the facial skin from halfway down the forehead to below the chin remained, the ears gone as well. The eyes were missing. *Eaten,* he surmised. Michael turned away and threw up, dropping to his knees, lurching forward, his abdomen heaving.

"People," he whispered as he wiped the vomit and dirt from the Stalker. "But not people like me. Cannibals."

*****

Suddenly, Michael sat up in the bed. His right arm out in front of him as if he still held the Stalker, his body covered in sweat. He realized he was holding his breath and slowly released it. Quietly, he moved out of the bed, not waking Natalia. He slid his feet into his house shoes next to the bed and slipped on his robe and moved silently down the stairs.

By the time he reached his study, his breathing was back to normal; almost anyway. He flicked on the light and walked to the desk. Sitting down he opened the bottom left drawer and pulled out a half bottle of Seagram's and a glass. Pouring the amber liquor into the glass, he noticed his hands were still shaking. He sat the bottle aside and took a sip.

"Another dream?" Natalia's voice came from the door way.

Looking up, Michael smiled and nodded. "Yeah. Same one, again."

"The cannibals?"

He nodded. Natalia walked over behind him and started messaging his neck and shoulders. "What's going on with you? That's the third time in as many weeks."

Michael shrugged. "Nerves I guess. Pretty big decisions ... uncertain futures for all of us," he said, taking another sip as he held out his right hand and saw the quivering had stopped.

Natalia spun the chair around and placed her hands on his cheeks. "Michael, our futures have always been uncertain. I can't make your demons go away any more than you can make mine leave. But together we are stronger than they are."

Michael pulled her down to sit on his lap. "I know. It's just..." his voice trailed off because he had no idea how to express his feelings.

She smiled. "It's just you want to make the right decisions. It's just you want everything to turn out okay. It's just the future hasn't been written and you are unsure. It's just you don't know where your father is or how to rescue him."

Michael pulled her close and she just held him to her breast for a long moment. Finally, he murmured, "Yeah, that about covers it." She didn't see the look in his eyes but felt his jaw muscles clinch.

Chapter Twenty-One

At nine o'clock the next morning, a tall slender man with an immaculate business suit walked into the Saint Germaine. The maitre de smiled. "May I help you?"

"Bob Yeager, is there a reservation for Tomlinson, John Tomlinson... is he here yet?"

"No, but right this way, Sir." The maitre de guided him to a secluded table next to the window in the back dining area. "May I get you something while you are waiting for your party?"

"Just coffee, black please."

Vale watched from across the street for ten minutes. He watched the street, the customers and the man sitting at the table. Nothing seemed out of place or out of the ordinary. With a mumbled, "What the hell," Vale got out of his car and walked inside.

Vale walked directly up to the tall slender man who stood and extended his right hand in greeting. Vale grabbed the hand in an overly developed grip and whispered, "Tomlinson, John Tomlinson, Mr. Yeager. A pleasure to meet you."

Croenberg/Yeager smiled his understanding. "It is my pleasure Mr. Tomlinson." Both men sat down.

Vale/Tomlinson said, "Your invitation mentioned you might wish to contribute to my enterprises."

Croenberg/Yeager smiled. "That's what I like... straight to business. Yes, I believe I can help your 'enterprises.'"

Vale/Tomlinson smiled. "Mr. Yeager... it is my pleasure. How did you hear of me, if I may ask?"

"Mr. Tomlinson, I am sure Mr. Greene shared my information with you. Although we have never met, I have followed your career with interest for several years. I have to say your latest endeavor in New Germany was masterful."

Vale/Tomlinson frowned. "New Germany... I'm afraid I do not know what you refer to."

"You are too modest Mr. Vale... I mean Tomlinson. I'm certain Mr. Burkholter and Mr. Freed appreciated your help."

Vale/Tomlinson's forehead furrowed but he kept the smile on his face. *I will kill those two idiots for sharing my name without my permission,* he thought.

Croenberg/Yeager said, "I have made a habit of keeping the two aspects of my life separated and distinct. My public side has made me quite comfortable while my private life has kept my interests alive."

"And exactly what are those private interests?"

"The total, final and complete destruction of John Thomas Rourke, his family and last but not least... his country. I am ready to make a contribution to your enterprises right now as a way of showing both my trustworthiness and my fidelity. If you will give me a secure numbered account, I will transfer four million dollars to it for you to use as you wish by the time the waiter has taken our order."

Chapter Twenty-Two

After the transfer was completed and verified, the waiter brought their order. Vale/Tomlinson smiled and said, "Thank you Mr. Yeager for your generous contribution."

"There will be more Mr. Tomlinson, much more as I learn more about your plans."

Vale/Tomlinson smiled and was silent for a moment. He leaned forward and whispered, "I will tell you this Mr. Yeager, my organization is staged for a coup d'état, literally a 'blow of state,' or more accurately, a 'blow against the state.' There are three operational aspects of what is about to happen; two are subtle and unseen. The other, more dynamic and observable, is called Operation Vollmond and is being prepared for implementation even as we speak."

Croenberg/Yeager raised an eye brow and smiled and in a whisper asked, "Operation Vollmond… what does the full moon have to do with John Rourke and his family?"

"Ah, Herr Yeager you speak German. Yes, Vollmond in German; Full Moon in English. A time of change, of mystery… of foreboding?"

Croenberg/Yeager thought for a moment. "And of death and new beginnings?"

"Yes, Herr Yeager, the death of the Rourkes, and of their offsprings. We will attack John Rourke and every member of his family. They will become executed like the enemies they are. Without remorse or mercy. They will be easy targets with the political position Michael Rourke enjoys. Their very fame as so-called 'Saviors of Mankind' shall be their undoing. They have become so famous, so intertwined with the daily news… they have no way to hide. Their every move can be tracked by the very element designed for their protection; the Secret Service which we have infiltrated."

"And who shall be your hunters?"

"We have a select group already identified," Vale/Tomlinson said. "They are the ones that took down the government of New Germany and Wolfgang Mann."

Croenberg/Yeager stretched lazily and with a degree of discouragement in his voice said, "You are correct, I am a student of history. I know that while the assassination of President Mann was violent and purposeful and eliminated virtually the entire hierarchy of his government... you missed his wife, Sarah Rourke-Mann. Why should I lend my support to an activity with only a fifty percent success rate?"

Vale/Tomlinson bristled visibly at the comment. "Our movement will call for all Neo-Nazis to hunt down the Rourkes and the Jew, Paul Rubenstein. Eventually, we shall entice all Germans, even women and children, to throw themselves at the enemy. This plan is not some kind of a desperate, last ditch effort of ineffective violence by fanatics and crazy people, I assure you. We have years of planning invested in this. Operatives that have been positioned deep within all governments and agencies. We will not fail, we will destroy the Rourkes and open a new day. A day where the tenants of National Socialism shall finally and forever control the world."

Croenberg/Yeager said with a grin, "Are you sure you are not simply about to repeat the past?"

"We are not losing a war Mr. Yeager, we are starting one. We are ready to strike and no one knows we are about to. We do not have to operate on someone else's timeline; we are in control of the clock."

Croenberg/Yeager appeared to be growing bored. "Mr. Tomlinson, I don't need rhetoric. I want results. I want to know what you are planning and whether or not I need to ask for my money back. This is beginning to sound like the pipe dream of a radical."

Vale/Tomlinson's eyes flashed, his face and voice grew hard. "Pro-American government leaders will be assassinated, we have operatives that have insinuated themselves in each nation's political system. We already have members or surrogates established in several, and the complete set up will be completed by the end of this year. Once Operation Vollmond is implemented, within days there will be assassinations. Nation states that resist us will also face other acts of violence and sabotage of railroad tracks, schools; and in some cases, poisoning the water, food and liquor supply.

"We will stand ready to use the media to our advantage. Not only do we currently control many newspapers and magazines, we are staged to purchase media outlets such as radio and television networks, but by using private radio transmitters, pro-Nazi graffiti, and hell... we are even considering dropping pro-Nazi leaflets when it is appropriate. We believe that within eighteen months, we can control the governments of America, New Germany, England and the rest of Europe, Australia and the other 'civilized' nations."

Croenberg/Yeager smiled. "We shall see, Mr. Tomlinson. We shall see. For now, I shall support your efforts financially. Do not fail me however, understand?"

Vale/Tomlinson relaxed. "Our plan will be initiated with reports and radio and television broadcasts spreading the word of our operatives' exploits. Terror is a most effective tool for political expediency. By this summer, Operation Vollmond will have completed the development of an elite troop of operatives, some that operate secretly behind enemy lines, but many more that operate in the public eye as movers and shakers of a more modern nationalistic movement. They are coordinated to the specific desires of each, soon to be member countries of the Alliance."

"I assume by a given point in time, the brain washing, propaganda and media manipulation will have seduced a significant segment of the population of the remaining civilized world to promote a 'peaceful, positive, world government, dedicated to promoting individual national interests within a global construct'; whatever in the hell that is supposed to mean," said Croenburg/Yeager.

"Yes, and then the final, most subtle and unseen part of the plan—we establish what has been called The New World Order. It has been tried before but this time there actually is a small group of international elites that will control and manipulate governments, industry and media organizations worldwide."

"How?"

"Oh, actually it very simple, there are two primary tools we use. The first is the system of central banking that we have secretly constructed over the last fifty years. Although on the surface each country appears to have its own system of central banking, they are inexorably secretly linked."

Vale/Tomlinson smiled and continued, "There have been a multitude of cleverly engineered and false attacks we and our predecessors have used to manipulate the various national populations into supporting those banks to the point that we now have the ability with the flip of a switch to establish a grip on the world economy. We are capable of deliberately causing inflation and depressions at will."

"I know it has always been supposed that the people behind the New World Order were international bankers," Croenberg/Yeager interjected.

"Yes and it is true. A dedicated cabal began laying the final plans, almost seventy-five years ago. They knew none of them would live to see the fruits of their labor. And they knew success would require operating at a level of secrecy no one believed possible. In that manner they could create a multitude of Red Herring trails, should anyone ever suspect what was occurring under their very noses.

"Lastly, they realized that the only way the New World Order would actually survive was to implement a takeover not only of national and international banking systems, but of the very nations themselves. What was critical was absolute media control. The grandchildren of those original cabal members meet every year… it goes unreported. How is that possible you might ask? Simple, we have already insinuated ourselves in the media. Those who report the news, we own. Therefore even when discussions at our meetings include the economy, world affairs, war and in general, world policy… there is no news agency that we cannot keep from publishing or, for that matter, even knowing about our plans.

"Look, we realized it was necessary to conceive 'a state of war' for a stable economy."

"War is a part of the economy?" Croenberg/Yeager asked.

"Absolutely. Therefore, it was necessary to conceive a state of war for a stable economy. The government, we believe, cannot exist for any significant length of time without war. Nation states literally exist in order to wage war.

It, war, serves as a vital function of diverting collective aggression. We realized that in order to maintain the status quo while reaping the 'benefits' of war, we had to create things that brought about the economic functions of war without the destruction. We settled on what we call 'the games,' benign incidents where 'alternate enemies' scare the hell out of people with reports of pollution, climate control, social upheaval or whatever."

"But," Croenberg/Yeager said, shaking his head, "of all the other possibilities, why finances?"

"Simple, finances are ways of waging warfare without firing a shot. A central bank like the Federal Reserve is recognized as something that can promote economic stability. Everything is fine until we, my group, decides it is time for the scale to become extreme. In reality, we are quite benevolent. We not only allow normalcy, we encourage it until such point in time as it is to our benefit to cause a serious disruption. The only problem has always been this pesky American philosophy of freedom and individual rights and such. The Rourkes have become the banner children of that philosophy."

Vale/Tomlinson paused. "My point is, it doesn't matter anymore. We are positioned. We are ready and the beauty is no one suspects our plans even exist. When we decide to 'turn the key' in the space of a tick of the clock, everything will change and it cannot be changed back. Once we have control and certain organizations and individuals have been eliminated, we will never lose control.

"Here is the reality: a lasting peace is not going to naturally occur. It has to be scripted and manipulated because mankind's nature is not to be peaceful. Then it has to be managed, managed and directed so the peace does last. War has always been an unfortunate and seldom acknowledged part of an economy. Someone said, 'There is nothing so beneficial to a troubled economy than a nice little war.'

"We simply manage the 'distractions.' Keep the populace focused on minutia, conspiracy theories and false narratives to the point they never realize what is actually happening. War games you see. In the old days, before The Night of the War, Aliens and UFOs were used as war games. The old Air Force program called Project Blue Book cataloged and 'explained away' UFO sightings while another, called Project Blue Beam, was nothing more than a conspiracy theory alleging fake Alien landings had occurred in order to scare the public into whatever global system was suggested.

"Then the dollars generated by these war games and conspiracy theories were put to use in a more 'positive' way. The Central Bank process provided not only economic stability, but a way to manipulate the value of a currency allowing financial booms to go higher, and crashes to be milder. And it was done surreptitiously in most cases. The Central Bank could drive the price of money up and keep risky investments under control to make the crashes of the stock markets milder."

Vale/Tomlinson waved his hand as if terminating the meeting. "I could expound of the process in greater depth but I believe you have the idea."

Chapter Twenty-Three

Croenberg walked out of the cafe and continued down Ala Moana Boulevard for several blocks, the weather was nice and the walk enjoyable. Two of Vale's operatives followed him at a distance. Vale had a reputation of not trusting people he did not control.

Croenberg turned into a large four story shopping mall and rode the escalator up to the third floor. One operative followed after a few moments on the escalator while the other rode up on the glass encased elevator on the far side of the mall. By the time they rejoined on the third floor there was a problem.

The taller one in a dark suit, asked with a threatening tone, "Don't tell me you lost him?"

"You're the one that lost him; the Boss isn't going to like this," the other one in casual clothes said.

"There he is going into the restroom," the taller one said. "You wait outside, don't let anyone in. I'll go in with him." Jogging over to the restroom the taller man entered, took a look around, stepped back out and said, "Must be in a stall."

The one is casual clothes said, "You know what the Boss said. If something didn't feel right, take the guy out. This is not feeling right to me."

"Or me. Guard the door. I'll be right back," the tall guy said and went back inside. Still no one was in view. He knelt down looking beneath the bottom of the stall doors for legs. Nothing. "What the…" the man whispered as he walked to the first stall door. He drew a .357 revolver and pushed the door open… nothing.

Second door, nothing. Third door, nothing; only one door left. He hit the door with his shoulder and moved inside. Another man, a younger man in a jogging suit, was crouching on the toilet. He straightened up and flashed a right front kick to the tall man's chin. His head snapped back and he went down, the revolver sliding across the restroom floor.

The younger man stepped off the toilet and knelt by the unconscious tall man. He touched the man's neck, found a pulse, then patted the man's cheek and whispered, "Sleep tight." He picked up the revolver and stuck it in the backpack he wore. Opening the door to leave the restroom, he spotted the other tail but ignored him.

The other man paid no attention, he was focused on finding the guy they were tailing and waited for his friend. After almost ten minutes of telling people the toilet had overflowed and the floor was a mess, he peeked inside. The tall man was just regaining consciousness.

The younger man walked briskly across the mall to the North parking lot, jogged a short distance and climbed into a white sports car. Driving normally, he exited the parking lot and was two miles down the road before he removed the wig and latex mask. Otto Croenberg rubbed the residue of rubber cement from the edges of his face and neck.

Chapter Twenty-Four

Michael and Shaw sat in the back seat of the Presidential limousine with the divider separating the driver from the passengers closed. Michael asked, "Alright, how much time did Croenberg say we have before this monstrosity is released on mankind?"

Shaw shook his head. "Not long, a few months at worst. End of the year at best. They want to build a momentum and tie it to the New Year. Sort of a New Year for the entire world message."

"That does not leave us much time."

"Croenberg said that Vale's hit teams normally operate in four-person teams. Their main armament includes fire and bullet resistant coats and clothing, silenced rifles and pistols. They are competent in everything from explosives, sniping attacks, arson, sabotage and assassination. They have been trained in the making of home-made explosives, manufacturing detonators from common articles such as pencils and a can of soup, and every member was to be trained in how to jump into a guard tower and strangle a sentry in one swift movement, using a wire garrote. When necessary multiple teams may merge when they are after a large number of targets, or a single one that is considered above average in difficulty to take out.

"I personally believe," Shaw continued, "estimates of over a hundred hit teams have been greatly exaggerated and I'm not sure how effective they would be as a part of an overall fighting force. While each team could be an effective guerilla unit, tying them together would be an exercise in trying to structure malcontents and ego maniacs into a single unit. They would, however, be effective as part of a Neo-Nazi 'underground railroad,' facilitating travel along certain routes and escape routes they call 'ratlines' that facilitate the movement of operatives and other Neo-Nazis throughout the world."

The limousine pulled up to the White House and the two men exited and headed to their respective offices.

Chapter Twenty-Five

Sarah and Emma walked past the Secret Service vehicle. "Good morning gentlemen. We are going down to the beach for a while," Sarah said as they passed.

The waves had whitecaps and the wind coming from offshore bore a chill even though it was late May. In blue jeans and jackets, they walked. Emma spoke first. "The chill is really in the air today."

Sarah nodded. "Yes, that front moved in last night and it will be like this for a day or two." They walked along again in silence for several minutes. "Emma..." Sarah stopped and could not find the words.

"Sarah, thank you for not asking, 'How are you?' I hurt... I hurt so bad I could die. In fact I wish I could die." Emma was silent and stood looking out at the waves. "No, that is not true. I don't want to die. I just don't want to hurt anymore. That's not the same thing, is it?"

Sarah shook her head. "No, no it isn't." Then she sighed. "Would you look at us? Two women who have loved and been married to the same man trying to console each other. What are the chances we would have ended up as friends?"

Emma smiled. "But we are friends, Sarah. You've lost your husband and I can't find mine. We both loved little Eddie and we both lost him. Very few women have shared as much as you and I have; the good and the bad."

"The good and the bad..." Sarah said. "My life wasn't supposed to turn out like this. My world wasn't supposed to end. My children weren't supposed to grow up without me. I was supposed to grow old and be a Grandma, baking cookies and smelling of flour and flowers..."

"Yes," Emma said. She had no idea of what else to say.

Sarah wiped away a tear. "You know... sometimes I wish we had never survived The Night of the War. I wished John had been home with us that day and it all could have ended with us as a family." She looked at Emma, "It would have been..."

Emma smiled. "It would have been NORMAL?"

"Yes," Sarah said still looking out to sea. "It would have been normal."

Emma took Sarah's hand. "But we would have never met, and I wouldn't have you as my friend. My children and your grandchildren would have never been born. So many things would never have happened; bad and good."

"Bad and good…" Sarah said. "Boy, aren't we a pair. I'm supposed to be helping you feel better and you're taking care of me."

Emma pulled Sarah close. "No Sweetie, we're taking care of each other."

Sarah pushed back. "What was … was that a shot?"

Emma looked back up the street a hundred yards away at the Secret Service vehicle that had paced them as they walked. The driver was slumped over the driver side door. Even at that distance she could see his brown suit coat was soaked with blood. The right front door was open and the other agent was running toward them, motioning for them to get down. He stumbled, went erect and collapsed in a pile. The women ran to him. "Get his radio and run!" Sarah shouted.

Emma checked for a pulse, snagged the radio and took off. Sarah pulled the .45 automatic from the dead man's hands and two extra magazines from his belt. She pulled a .38 snub nosed revolver and one 5-round speed strip from an ankle holster and followed Emma. They sprinted to a dune about twenty yards away and dropped down behind it. "Here," Sarah said handing Emma the .38 and the speed strip. "You only have ten rounds total, Emma. Make them count."

Emma opened the .38's cylinder, confirmed a full load of five rounds and stuck the speed strip in her pocket. Sarah was trying to raise the Secret Service detail on the radio but no one was answering. She switched frequencies. "HPD, HPD this is an emergency. Please respond."

"Go ahead emergency caller, what is the emergency?"

"We have two Secret Service agents down. This is Sarah Rourke-Mann, I have Emma Rourke with me and we are under attack."

"Location?"

Sarah looked around, got her bearings and said, "Three hundred yards, east of John Rourke's beach front home." A bullet zinged past Sarah's head, kicking up sand behind her. "Hurry, hurry please, we are under fire. We are on the beach behind a sand dune. Hurry, please hurry."

Emma glanced over the sand dune. "They're coming Sarah." Three men approached with semi-automatic weapons. They opened up and started chewing the beach and the sand dune to pieces. Sarah threw a snap shot at them; the .45 slug tore into the nearest man's throat. A fountain of blood spray appeared behind him. The return fire was so intense there was no way to fire again. The two women tried to shoot around the dune but were driven back. Emma took another look. "Another vehicle just pulled up."

Sarah nodded. "Then we are dead, Emma."

The long and loud stuttering of a heavy, fully automatic weapon reached the women. Then there was silence, followed by two burps of full automatic fire and a voice. "Sarah, Emma, it is safe to come out. Hurry, we must leave."

Sarah peeked around the dune ready for some kind of trap. Two bloody messes marked where the other two killers had been cut in half by the heavy weapon. A tall slender man with a long black rifle was changing magazines. "Hurry" he said and removed his cap.

"Otto, is that you?" Sarah shouted.

"Yes, hurry."

"Come on Emma, follow me," she said and ran toward Croenberg. As they passed, he threw her the keys. "Start my car; I'll be there in a second." The two women ran to the sedan; Emma got in the back seat and Sarah the driver's seat. Croenberg followed quickly and hopped in the passenger seat. He had barely shut the door when Sarah jammed the gas pedal to the floor and took off.

"Don't go back to the highway," Croenberg said. "Emma, what was John's back up escape route?"

Emma shouted and pointed, "Turn left four blocks up, jump the curb and follow the beach for a quarter mile then turn right. That will carry us out to a back road which goes to the Marina." Sarah spun the wheel. A car appeared behind them.

Sarah shouted, "Here they come again! Black sedan coming up behind us, very fast!"

"Pull over, now!" Croenburg shouted.

Sarah slammed on the brakes and cut the wheel to the right. Croenberg was out of the car and laid the automatic rifle across the roof. He took a deep breath, and let a little out, aimed, and began to fire single action shots at the approaching vehicle, still a hundred yards away. Small arms fire from the approaching car ricocheted off the bulletproof body and glass of Croenberg's sedan. He continued to fire deliberate shots, one bullet hitting the radiator, steam pouring from the grill. His next shot ricocheted off the wind screen. The next one penetrated the glass and tore through the driver's face.

Blood, bone and brains sprayed into the back seat. The vehicle stopped. Croenberg reached into his pocket for the last 25-round magazine as three doors opened and three assault rifles started blazing away at him. With precision, Croenberg dropped the two shooters on the right side of the vehicle. The last one turned to run and made it about thirty steps before Croenberg's last slug intersected the man's zigzag path and sliced through his spine, sending bone shards tearing through his heart.

Croenberg took a final look and said, "Let's go." Sarah rose up from the seat, put the car in Drive and took off again. A block later, she hopped the curb, took a left and kicked sand up behind her for a quarter mile.

Emma shouted, "Turn right Sarah just past that electric pole, then follow the easement to the Marina!"

Chapter Twenty-Six

Shaw charged into the President's office unannounced. "Michael, we have to leave… right now!"

Michael was taken aback; it was the first time Tim Shaw had addressed him by his first name while on duty. Michael followed him out. Once they were out of the building, Michael said, "Okay, Tim… what's going on?"

"There was an attack at your father's place. I have two agents and seven alleged bad guys down at the scene; all dead. Emma and your mother are missing. A silver colored sedan was reported leaving the area at a high rate of speed driving west along the beach front. I've ordered HPD to seal off the Marina with choppers, boats and vehicular patrols. They are to keep the east side of the bay locked down until we get there."

"Silver colored sedan, huh? High rate of speed?"

"Yeah, sound like anybody we know?"

Michael nodded. "Damn, I sure hope so."

"I've got the keys to the Beast and with your permission, I'm driving," Tim said.

Michael jogged down the hallway to keep up with Shaw. "Sure, but why the Presidential limousine?"

Tim said, "Closest thing we have to a tank should one be needed and a hell of a lot faster."

Chapter Twenty-Seven

Shaw got the call as they pulled out onto the thoroughfare. Taking a deep breath, he said into the phone, "Now say that again, slowly."

"Mr. Shaw, this is Captain Harrison from HPD Tactical. There has been an attack at John Rourke's beach front property. Mrs. Rourke and Mrs. Rourke-Mann are missing. We have two of your agents and three UNSUBS dead at the beach. One of the UNSUBS died from a .45 slug, which is what your men carried and one of their service weapons and a backup .38 are missing. There are four more dead and a vehicle disabled a few blocks away."

Shaw took a deep breath before speaking in measured tones. "Captain Harrison, I have already heard about it. I'm not sure if you are aware of this fact but Mrs. Rourke happens to be my daughter and Mrs. Rourke-Mann is the President's mother, and he and I are enroute as we speak."

"Yes Sir, I am."

"Good, then you better have every helicopter and patrol vehicle combing that area and the ocean covered by patrol boats. If you don't... you better have by the time I get there."

"Already have that, Mr. Shaw. Witnesses saw a silver sedan driving at a high rate of speed away from the area."

Shaw perked up. "What direction was it headed in?"

"Jumped the curb and headed west on the beach."

"Captain, head to the Marina. Evacuate the Marina and block off the area on the east side of the bay... lock it down and stay put. Tell me where your Command Post is set up, the President and I will be there shortly. Do not, I repeat... do not attempt to approach the east side of the bay. Your men will be cut down."

"We're set up in the parking lot of the Baptist Church on the corner of 5th and Elm. Mr. Shaw, I assure you my men..."

"Captain," Shaw interrupted, "let me assure you if you and your men do not follow my orders exactly... If you or your men make a single mistake that results in any harm to my daughter or the President's mother..." Shaw took a deep breath to calm down. "Well, if that happens, whoever screws up better eat their gun because when we get there, I'll shove it up his ass and pull the trigger myself!"

Tim turned to Michael. "Sir, this is where you get out. I'm not putting you in danger. I'll drop you at the perimeter with the Captain. I'll come to you, once I have our girls back."

Chapter Twenty-Eight

The silver sedan was parked in front of 447 Beach Front Lane on the east side of the bay. Two doors further up and across the street at 444 Beach Front Lane, the shades were drawn and the place looked abandoned. The grass had been allowed to grow wild and the place looked like it had never been landscaped. 444 had direct access to the bay and a boat house with a power boat if needed.

Inside 444, Sarah Rourke-Mann moved back and forth between windows on the north and east sides of the home. Emma Rourke patrolled the west and south sides while Otto Croenberg reloaded magazines and waited.

He doubted they would be there long but if things did not go according to his plan, 444 was well stocked with everything that could be needed in an emergency. The radio Sarah had taken from the dead agent had been quiet since their arrival. It squawked, "Emma, if you are secure move to Charlie Eight."

Otto picked up the radio and switched to channel eight. "Tim, this is Otto Croenberg. Do you read? Over."

"Affirmative, are the women alright? Over."

"Affirmative, the packages are secure, repeat the packages are secure. Over."

"Roger that, very good news. Are you ready for extraction? Any medical issues? Over."

"Affirmative on the first, negative on the second. I will expect you and you alone, in how many? Over."

"Roger, we have the area secure and a parameter established. I am on my way down; I'm in the 'Beast' and alone."

Otto smiled at the women. "Emma, your father is going to pick us up. Ladies our ride is on its way down, let's get ready to move. Seems we get the bomb proof, bullet proof Presidential limousine for our trip out."

Chapter Twenty-Nine

Michael, Paul, Otto and Tim sat on Emma's patio. Natalia had taken Annie, Sarah and Emma inside and upstairs. "Okay guys… what the hell?" Shaw asked.

"It appears to have begun," Michael said, thinking the intelligence Otto had gathered during his undercover meeting with Vale was accurate… unfortunately. "It seems the hit teams are active. Otto, I want to thank you for what you did today."

"Unnecessary to thank me, Michael, but you are welcome."

Paul stood up. "Thanks anyway, Otto. If you hadn't been there… well we wouldn't be sitting here enjoying a glass of Seagram's and a good cigar. Point is, I agree with Michael… it has begun and we have to get ahead of it and quickly."

"As we learned with Wolfgang's death, no place is truly impregnable," Tim said. "I think secrecy is a better armor than thick walls right now. I have sent another team to the Rourke Survival Academy as another layer over the kids. I want your approvals to move Annie, Emma and Sarah to a secret, secure location until further notice or until it is time to make the final move. Whichever comes first."

"Yes, I agree," Paul said. "Had they gone after Annie first, we… I would have lost her today. Michael, I think it is time to put the plan in motion. I would like to leave tonight in order to be there tomorrow in time to take advantage of as much daylight as possible."

Michael nodded. "If your team is ready to go that quickly, I can get you there tonight. Otto, I want you and Tim to work together on the security for our ladies. You two agree on what you need and Tim will make it happen."

Otto reached in his pocket and pulled out a sheet of paper. "Timothy, I hope you do not mind that I have some suggestions to start with."

Tim smiled. "Otto, to be honest with you, I was not very happy when Paul and Michael approached me with the idea of you being 'overwatch' for Sarah.

Frankly, I thought you were too old to be effective in the field if trouble should start. Today you proved me wrong. You and I will be fine working together."

Otto smiled. "What is that saying you Americans have about old age…? 'I'm not as good as I once was but I'm as good once as I ever was?'"

Both men laughed. Shaw said, "That's it Otto, I think you and I both fit that description. I look forward to working with you."

Otto Croenberg, former President of the Democratic German Republic, former Neo-Nazi, stood up straight and clicked his heels together, bent from the waist and stuck out his right hand to Shaw. "And Timothy, I look forward to working with you."

Michael took a last puff on the cigar and snubbed it out. Reaching for his drink he slugged the rest of it down. "Then gentlemen, you have to excuse me. I have to collect the wife and kick in the plans necessary to save us all and, hopefully, this country."

Chapter Thirty

General Sullivan and Jose Zima walked out into the hanger, looked around and walked over to Rodney Thorne. "General Thorne," Zima said, "we need to coordinate with you and the ship's sensors."

"Sure, Sir. What are you looking for?"

"Well, that depends entirely on what your ship sensors can do," Sullivan replied. "We need to see what, if anything, it can detect underground and at what distance."

Thorne shook his head. "Can't say, Sir. Haven't used The Egg to search or test for stuff like that. Can you tell me anything more about what you're looking for?"

"The Egg, is that what you named it?" Zima asked.

Thorne grinned. "Seemed appropriate with its shape. What am I looking for?"

Zima shook his head but continued, "A very large object about one hundred meters underground that generates a pretty substantial electrical field."

"That will be a big help," Thorne said, smiling. "The ship doesn't have X-ray vision or anything like that but I know it is pretty sensitive to electrical impulses. May not be able to show you what it is or what it looks like, but it should be able to pin down where it is. Do you have a search area?"

"We do but I don't want to pin it down too closely," Sullivan explained. "Frankly, I'm not too sure about this data; could be a Red Herring. How about we give you some search perimeters and you see if you can hone in on it?"

"No problem. When and where do you want me to take a look?"

Sullivan gave Thorne a handwritten note. "As soon as possible. Memorize these coordinates then destroy the note. Look them up yourself but do it confidentially. I want you to follow the same parameters you did on the weapons test flight. Understand?"

"No footprints or bread crumbs, right?"

"Exactly," Sullivan said. "No telling who is watching and we don't want to give them any clues that we're looking."

"I'm already scheduled for a flight in two days," Thorne said. "It's been announced so it would probably be better to stick to that schedule rather than chance the media getting wind of it. How about I 'slip the surly bonds of earth' and go 'where never lark or even eagle flew?'"

"General, you wax poetic," Zima said. "With apologies to John Gillespie Magee, how about you just see if you get a hit anywhere in that area."

Chapter Thirty-One

Sullivan sat at the desk in his study looking at the picture of him and his wife on their wedding day. "Well, Baby Girl, here's to you, Angel," he said, taking a sip of Scotch whiskey from a special bottle. She had given him the bottle as an early gift for their twenty-third wedding anniversary. She died two months before that anniversary and the bottle had never been opened... until today.

A tear rolled down his left cheek as he said quietly, "Need to talk to you Honey. Got some decisions to make and I need your help." He took another sip; the dark liquid felt good going down his throat and warming his insides. "Here's the deal..." He talked to the picture for the next several hours laying out the issues and problems. He and she had done the same thing many times while she was alive; this was the first time he had done it since she died.

When he stopped, he was smiling. "Thanks Baby Girl. I love you, as much as always," he said as he slugged back the last of his drink and corked the bottle. He went into the bottom right drawer of his desk; files hung suspended on a rack inside the drawer. Thumbing through them he found the one he wanted and pulled it out. Laying it on the desk he pulled a legal tablet and pencil out. An hour and a half later, he had several pages of notes and a stack of military discharge reports and civilian resumes.

He leaned back and picked up the receiver on the desk phone and dialed his personal aide. "Yes, General. Everything alright? I don't usually hear from you this late in the evening unless something is wrong."

"No Harvey, everything is alright. I need you to do three things for me."

"Yes Sir, what do you need?"

"When you get a minute come upstairs, I want you to find some phone numbers and contact information for some people. That's the first thing."

Harvey Bishop had pulled out a note pad. "The second thing?"

"I want you be very quiet about it, nothing overt and definitely don't raise any flags."

Bishop made a note. "Am I to assume I give the information directly to you and I don't know nothing about it?"

Sullivan smiled into the phone. "You don't know anything."

"What's the third thing, Sir?"

"Bring two cigars and meet me on the patio, Harvey."

"We smoking or we drinking?"

"Both," Sullivan said, smiling. "I broke open that special bottle Baby Girl gave me."

Bishop was quiet for a moment not sure what to say. Finally he decided he wouldn't say anything and hung up. Harvey Bishop had been handpicked by Frank Sullivan as his aide. In accordance with protocol, a four-star General is known as the General of the branch of the service he or she is in, better known as the Chief of Staff, or COS, USA.

As such, COS is authorized a full colonel, one lieutenant colonel and one major to serve as his *aides-de-camp*. Harvey Bishop was not one of the aides-de-camp. He was not a commissioned officer as the aides-de-camp must be. He was an NCO, a Non Commissioned Officer. Years ago, he had saved Sullivan's life during a scrape in one of the border wars in the Continental United States.

Then Colonel Sullivan's command had suffered heavy losses. One of the Army translators had sold the unit out and when the ambush was sprung, it was devastating. When the re-enforcements arrived, the battle scene was horrific... and Sullivan was nowhere to be found. The survivors were airlifted to the nearest base with a hospital and the bodies of the dead were recovered.

Four days later, a wounded Sergeant First Class Harvey Bishop walked up to a guard post at a Forward Operating Base nicknamed Fort Apache, dragging a travois with a nearly dead Frank Sullivan on it. Both men survived and became fast friends and when Sullivan was promoted to Brigadier General, he had Bishop promoted to Sergeant Major and later Command Sergeant Major and assigned to him. When Bishop's age, several years older than Sullivan, prevented his participation in the field, Sullivan named him as his personal aide and they had been together ever since.

Chapter Thirty-Two

Michael Rourke, General Sullivan and Paul Rubenstein sat in the conference room. "Mr. Rubenstein," Sullivan said, "you are the only one here that is old enough to remember much about the time before The Night of the War. It sounds to me like we are about to repeat that period in our history."

Paul cleared his throat and looked around the table. "I was born in 1953 and have just a few memories of life in the 1950s; hopefully, most of them are accurate. I remember being issued a pair of military style dog tags by the Board of Education. Several Boards of Education across the country considered the world beyond the immediate neighborhood dangerous, and thought it necessary to issue dog tags to identify students in case of a devastating bomb attack from Cold War enemies of the United States.

"I remember being a student in kindergarten and elementary school. That was a time when kids walked to school with friends, without parental supervision. When we lived off base, I could walk to the supermarket to buy a loaf of bread for my mother. It was something I liked to do, and there were virtually no safety concerns.

"I remember the shelter drills and air raid drills we did in school. I don't think I understood the ramifications; they just broke up the day and gave us a break from class. We did the 'duck and cover' thing as well as lining up in the halls and keeping away from the glass doors and windows that could shatter on us. These were just part of the school day. What terrified me were the air raid sirens.

"There were public service messages that aired on TV, these sometimes warned parents to send small children out of the room so they wouldn't be frightened by what was about to be shown. When I got sent out I'd watch from a place out of my parents' sight. These were mostly about what would happen when a nuclear bomb exploded. There was a scene I'll never forget about sleeping people melting in their beds. In spite of all this, I had a relatively normal childhood. I was more traumatized by teenage heartbreak and bullies growing up than anything."

Turning to Michael Rourke, Sullivan asked, "Do you remember the term CONELRAD?"

"No, what was it?"

Sullivan looked at his notes. "CONELRAD stood for Control of Electromagnetic Radiation. It was a method of emergency broadcasting to the public in the event of enemy attack. It was intended to allow continuous broadcast of civil defense information to the public using radio or TV stations, while rapidly switching the transmitter stations to make the broadcasts unsuitable for Soviet bombers who might attempt to hone in on the signals. That was actually a fear during World War II, when German radio stations, based in or near cities, were used as beacons by pilots of bombers.

"It's not important, just a favorite historical note of mine. While it was practiced a lot, by the time The Night of the War came, it had been replaced by the Emergency Broadcast System. Unlike its successors, CONELRAD was never intended to be used for severe weather warnings or local civil emergencies."

Michael took control of the meeting. "Gentlemen, we are getting off topic. You have to make some decisions and unfortunately there is not a lot of time. I have explained what I plan for myself and my family. However with the threat analysis by General Sullivan and our inside man, there is not a lot of time."

No one outside of Michael, Tim Shaw and Paul Rubenstein knew yet that Michael was referring to Otto Croenberg.

Chapter Thirty-Three

"Here you go Sir," Bishop said and handed a list to Sullivan. "I found all but three of them. Don't know where they are today but I suspect they are in places where they didn't want to be found."

Sullivan studied the names. "Hmmm, yeah I see what you mean with those three. They are either hiding out from angry wives or angry husbands. Harvey, I want you to reach out to these people. Don't pressure anyone, just tell them I'd like for them to come to a meeting and hear me out. They'll have a week to put their affairs in order to come to the first meeting. Then we will give them two weeks to come back or drop the whole thing. Either way it has to be their choice. No pressure, no fowl, no matter which way they go. I don't have firm dates yet, tell them you'll get back to them in a few days. Right now, I just need to know how many are interested. Can you do that?"

Bishop nodded. "I can, may I ask the General what is going on?"

"You can ask Sergeant Major, but I can't tell you much right now. Let's see how we do on Phase One—making contact with these folks, explaining the plan to them and finding out how many want to play our game."

"Okay, and Phase Two is where I get to ask questions?"

"No Harvey, that will be in Phase Three. All I can tell you right now is you have a seat at the table, a hand in this game if you want to do it."

"Hell, General," Bishop said as he turned to leave. "That's the only question I had. Was I going with you?"

"How long have you had my back, Harvey?"

"Damn General, you don't have to hurt my feelings by reminding me how old the two of us are," Bishop said, slamming the door on his way out. Sullivan looked at his watch, 0917 hours. He smiled.

"Okay, that's what we'll call this thing, Unit 917. Gives it a name without giving out any information." He closed the file and wrote UNIT 917 across the top in bold letters.

Chapter Thirty-Four

Thorne climbed into The Egg and settled in. He had spent several hours the night before going over the view screen that helped him operate the ship. Without manual controls, like a throttle and a stick, learning the capabilities of the ship was difficult. He had learned he had to get "smarter" than the ship to know what to ask of it.

He was focused on two sensor programs: one for electrical influence and one for magnetic field distortion. He still had no idea what he was searching for and he figured one or both of those might not help him find that "missing needle," but might just locate the hay stack it was in.

He buckled on his new communications unit. While he was much more comfortable with the craft, he knew it was necessary to record all of his flights in case something happened and another pilot had to pick up the pieces if he died. He also had the ability with this unit to take pictures of the hologram screen. He cleared his throat and settled down to business. "Research Craft One, Comm check. Over."

"Comm check, roger, Research One. We read you 5 x 5. Over."

"Roger, Research One, requesting permission to launch. Over."

"Roger, Research One. You have permission, good luck. Over."

Thorne positioned his hands on the control pad and thought, *Systems on.* The holographic image sprang to life. *Ship integrity check.* It showed sealed. *Power on, Cloak on.* There was an almost indiscernible whine as The Egg powered itself up. *Launch sequence activate, go to cruising speed of 450, altitude 20,000 feet.*

The silver, egg-shaped vehicle sprang into the air, climbing quickly. For thirty minutes or so, he followed the standard protocol. The Egg was handling normally. "Research One to tower. Over."

"Go ahead, Research One. Over."

"Research One, control and speed checks completed. You guys have all of the telemetry I presume. Over."

"Roger, Research One. You are cleared for the second phase. Over."

"Roger, Research One, climbing. I will check in with you in twenty minutes. Over."

Thorne increased speed by twenty-five percent and set The Egg on a new course and heading; up. He followed a course that had been worked out by scientists and was designed to keep the bulk of the planet between him and the ships belonging to the KI who were in a geo synchronic orbit over Antarctica. Additionally, this path kept him clear of any orbiting satellites or observation-listening stations of other governments. He watched both the clock and the flight path screen.

In order to keep a record of the flight, he spoke into the communications unit after giving his mental command. "Sensors on. Electrical influence and magnetic disturbance scan." Waves of rippling lights played across the hologram screen. A series of numbers appeared adjacent to the areas of most activity. These began to subside the further north he went. Once above the southern edge of the Polar Glaciers, they stopped almost entirely. He had anticipated they would.

He altered his course slightly to the northwest and continued on. Eighteen minutes into the flight the hologram screen flared up into active mode. He activated his Communications unit camera and shot five pictures in quick succession and said, "Sensors off." Two minutes later, he spoke into the unit again.

"Tower, this is Research One. Over."

"Go ahead, Research One. Over."

"Tower, this is Research One ..."

BLAM, BLAM! The craft was slammed sideways, twice—to the right and then back to the left. Thorne scanned the screen for readouts that would explain what had happened; nothing. Confused, Thorne mentally increased the speed and changed the attitude of the craft, it shot almost straight up. He focused on the hologram screen. *EXPAND VIEW,* he mentally ordered and immediately saw the problem. Two blips on the screen approaching from his six o'clock.

"Tower, this is Research One, I am taking fire, repeat I am taking fire. I have been engaged by two unidentified craft. Breaking the atmosphere now, need some room to operate."

For a moment, the communications unit was silent. A deep baritone voice Thorne recognized as Sullivan came on, "Research One, are you damaged? Over."

"Tower, negative. Ship's hull has maintained integrity. I have evaded the threat for the moment. Over."

"Research One, weapons status? Over."

"Tower, weapons online and ready. Over."

"Research One … you are cleared to return fire if necessary. Copy, Research One? Over."

"Copy Tower."

BLAM! Thorne shook from the impact but all systems were still in the green.

"Tower, it just became necessary… going to be a little busy, check back with you in a few. Over." *Dive,* Thorne thought and The Egg shot downward. *Okay, let's see if you guys are any good. Wonder if you have had any dogfight training.*

Thorne had to get the advantage; his best position was to get above or behind the opponent. Trouble was he had two bogies on his butt. Had he been in a cockpit, he would have watched over his shoulder anticipating when the bogie behind would fire and then break left or right. He edged slightly to the left, moving directly in front of that bogie and slowing slightly. Thorne gave a slow count of "One, two, three," then commanded the craft to climb.

His next command was, "Increase speed, roll to the left," and his craft inverted to complete a circle. The craft behind him followed. With a laugh Thorne said, "Didn't expect that one, did you Pal? If you liked that, try this."

The bogie to the right was slower to react. Thorne said, "Weapons system." Three categories jumped into view: blast, burst, trickle. "Trickle, right. Two o'clock, a thousand yards, continuous fire," he said. A steady stream of energy leapt from the nose of his craft; the slower craft behind him was caught in the beam and vaporized.

"Now, you bastard, it's just you and me," he said aloud to the other enemy craft. "Dive," he said and re-entered the atmosphere and slowed as the other craft closed on him. Thorne was close enough to see the enemy craft on his view screen. "Well, well," he said. "Look who dropped in to play."

Thorne had already learned that many of the limitations of the jets he had flown were nonexistent in The Egg; things like gravity and thrust-to-weight ratio didn't matter anymore. What did matter was the craft's kinetic energy—a function of its mass, speed, potential energy, gravity and altitude combined to make up the "energy package."

A fighter flying at low altitude but at high speed may have the same total energy as a fighter of equal mass, but flying at a low speed and high altitude. Thorne continued his dive. The pilot who can maintain the higher energy package will usually have the advantage. There were three other factors that often decided the outcome of a dogfight: experience, luck and the ability to act instantaneously when an advantage opened up.

As soon as he hit the clouds he increased speed and made a lateral 360 degree turn to the left. His enemy was now in front of him. *Blast, one from nose,* Thorne thought and a single surge of green energy erupted from the nose of the craft, passing just below the enemy craft. He saw the pilot react and immediately go into a climb to escape. But Thorne had started his own climb as soon as he had fired. "Burst, one thousand yards off port." Another green surge launched and smashed into the other craft. It shuddered and fell away to the right; Thorne closed for the kill.

The bogie wobbled and staggered back to level flight. At 12,000 feet Thorne leveled off and watched him up ahead. The bogie began a slow acceleration, he was definitely damaged. Thorne closed to a thousand yards, checked his scope for any surprises and finding none said out loud, "Slow now, I've got time."

As the craft filled the enemy craft and started to turn left, Thorne said, "Blast one from the nose." The craft shuddered in flight. "Blast another one from the nose." The craft slowed and smoke began to trail it. "Blast one more from the nose." The enemy craft exploded.

"Tower, this is Research One. I am returning to base. Is Baker-Baker still there? Over."

Sullivan's voice came back, "Research One, yeah, I'm still here. Threat analysis. Over."

"Two bogies, Baker-Baker. Splashed both of them. Over."

"Research One, could you identify? Over."

"Roger that, Sir, and you ain't gonna like it. Research One. Out."

*****

Thorne exited The Egg and walked with a slight limp over to where General Sullivan and Jose Zima stood. Removing his communications unit, he took out a computer chip and handed it to Sullivan. "Here ya go, Boss. I think I found what you were looking for, where you were expecting me to. And I found something neither of us expected."

Sullivan noticed a trickle of blood from Thorne's nose. "Are you okay, General?" Sullivan touched his own nose. Thorne got the hint and pulled a handkerchief from the pocket on the leg of his flight suit. "Yeah, I'm fine. Just took some rattling up there."

Zima took the chip from Sullivan and placed it in a slot on the side of a portable scanner with a display screen. Zima hit a switch and the screen coalesced into a display. He checked the numbers and the data. "He's right General Sullivan. He found the target exactly where our reports put it." Zima scrolled through to the end of the recording. "And... he found this."

Sullivan looked at the screen, frowned then smiled and turned to his aide. "Get me the President on the phone. And have General Thorne transported immediately to Tripler for a full medical work up."

*****

Sullivan made a secure call to Michael Rourke. "Sir, we have a problem. Need to brief you on something."

"Go ahead, General."

"Not on the phone, Sir. I'm requesting a meeting with you and the senior staff as soon as possible."

Michael frowned and thought, *I don't know who I can trust. Maybe there are moles on my staff.* "General, several of my top people are unavailable. Would it be acceptable to brief me and if it is necessary I can recall them and schedule a time for you to personally brief them?"

"That will work, Sir. I'm on my way to you," Sullivan said as he hung up.

Chapter Thirty-Five

"Appreciate your time, Mr. President, especially on such short notice," Sullivan said.

"Not a problem, Frank. What is so urgent?"

For the next ten minutes Sullivan spoke uninterrupted while Michael Rourke took notes. When Sullivan was finished, Michael laid down his pen and walked to the window. For several moments he stood like a statue looking out over the south lawn. The President took a deep breath in and let it out in a "Whew. Those are pretty significant things. How do you want to proceed?"

Sullivan removed the unlit cigar he had been chewing on and said, "Sir, first of all, I need to make contact with The Keeper. Is he still in town?"

"Yes he is."

"Second, I want to read David Blackman into this. And third I want to recall some of the 442nd members from the mission they are on."

Michael turned around and looked at Sullivan for a long minute. "Okay, I'll get the meeting set up with The Keeper. Where do you want him?"

"The secure medical ward at Ambrose Federal Detention Center."

Michael sat down and said, "Done." He reviewed his notes. "Read Blackman in on this, I assume you want him to interview the 442nd folks?"

"Yes Sir, probably both him and The Keeper?"

"Do it," Michael said. "Now Frank, tell me more about this pyramid Thorne found."

Sullivan opened his briefcase, pulled out a file and handed it to the President. Michael started reading, stopped and looked at Sullivan. He opened the center drawer to his desk, removed a crystal ash tray and handed it to Sullivan. "General, will you light that damn cigar or throw it away. You're chewing it to pieces."

Sullivan fished out an old Zippo and rolled the striker wheel, put it to the end of the cigar and puffed. With a smile he said, "Thank you Sir." He carried the ashtray over to the outside door, cracked it open and blew a lung full of smoke outside. He had the ash tray full of ashes by the time Michael finished the file. He snubbed the cigar out in the crystal ash tray and sat it on the table.

Michael was silent. He turned his chair around and stared out the window off into the distance. Finally, he went back into his center desk drawer, pulled something out and stood. "Walk with me, General." Together they went out that side door and started across the lawn. Sullivan adjusted his saucer cap and matched Michael's stride but didn't speak. Michael handed Sullivan one of the cigars he had pulled from his desk. He bit off the end of another and turned to Sullivan. "Got a light?"

Sullivan smiled. "Didn't know you smoked, Sir."

Michael puffing the cigar to life said, "Don't usually, Frank. Am I correct you're thinking the pyramid is where the Aliens are holding my father?"

Sullivan had his cigar going and looked back across the lawn at the White House. "Don't know for sure, Sir. Maybe." Michael nodded and drew on the cigar. "I'm going to be honest with you, Mr. President. There is a lot going on right now that doesn't make sense to me."

Michael snorted a laugh. "Welcome to my world Frank and drop the Sir. We're just two guys right now enjoying a cigar together. Permission to speak freely, as you G.I.s say."

Sullivan smiled. "Roger that, Michael." Sullivan took another drag and let the smoke drift from his nostrils as he spoke. "Here's the deal, I'm getting vibes from a lot of sources that say several folks, including some in Congress and several elsewhere, are making noises about taking over. Now, we find this damn pyramid and while we're doing that, Thorne gets attacked by the KI."

"Yeah, yeah I know," Michael said. "I'm hearing the same thing. I have been for some time but figured it was just talk. The attack on Belleview and Wolf's murder… maybe it isn't all talk. Look at what happened with my mother and Emma."

"How are they by the way?" Sullivan asked with genuine concern.

"Lucky, damn lucky… they have settled down pretty well. I think I'm more concerned than they are." Michael took another draw and let it out as he watched a cloud go by overhead. "Do you ever miss it, Frank?"

"Miss what?"

"Being in the field, right in the thick of things?"

Sullivan smiled sadly. "Yeah, yeah I do. While I'm good at the back office stuff, I'm better in the field. Closer to the men, there I can see the impact of what I do and what I didn't do. Up here in the Ivory Tower, I'm not sure whether or not I always get the truth. I wonder if people are telling me what I 'need' to hear or what they think I 'want' to hear. Make sense?" Michael nodded. "No disrespect meant but I get the feeling you have the same issues?"

Michael nodded again. "None taken and you are correct. There was a time I dealt with issues myself. Now there is an entire staff dedicated to keeping me from sticking my foot in my mouth."

Sullivan laughed. "Like the time you knocked Phillip Greene on his ass during the debate?"

Michael smiled, taking another draw on his cigar. "Yeah, man it felt good to bust that pompous bastard's bubble. Trouble is, it didn't do any good."

"Oh, you're wrong there, Boss," Sullivan smiled. "It won you the respect of a lot in the military, I'll tell ya. We get so tired of babysitting 'idiot' politicians who couldn't wipe their own asses. They lie every time their lips move or the polls shift. They hang us out to dry at the drop of a hat, then cut the benefits they promised and we worked our asses off for. It was a pleasure to see a real man deal with a bastard like Greene."

Michael looked at the cigar half gone in his hand. "Go ahead with what you want to do with The Keeper, Blackman and the 442nd. I want to know what results you get and… Frank, I can't underscore this enough. I want this all handled by you personally and you report directly to me and me only. Here's the other problem, besides maintaining as much secrecy as you can on what you're doing… I don't know how much time we have for you to get it done."

Sullivan frowned. "Anything I need to know about, Mr. President?"

Michael shook his head. "Not at this moment, General, but we'll probably need another cigar in a couple of days." Michael threw the cigar butt down and turned to go back to the White House.

Sullivan ditched his cigar and said, "I'll bring them next time, Boss."

Chapter Thirty-Six

As Sullivan stood watching the President of the United States walk back to the White House, he decided it was time to pitch the idea he'd been working on. As he had been trained to all of his life, he seized on relevant facts, a bucket of speculation, added a pinch of intuition and jogged after the President.

"Mr. President, hold up a minute."

Michael stopped and turned. "What is it, General?"

"Sir, do I still have your permission to speak freely?"

Michael nodded. "Certainly, go ahead."

"Okay, I have an idea… this is pretty rough… but I think it is a good idea."

Michael smiled. "Go ahead. Spit it out; if there's something there… we'll hammer out the details."

Sullivan nodded. "Personal security, mission optimization, trustworthiness."

Michael cocked his head. "I don't understand, General."

"Those are three things I concern myself about when I'm dealing with you, Sir. Your personal security, how to make the most out of each mission and who the hell can I trust to protect you and the mission."

Michael nodded, still not sure where Sullivan was headed. "Okay…"

"A special team. A unique platoon, not sure what to call it but go with the idea," Sullivan said. "A team of multi-faceted individuals with overlapping areas of expertise and experience. Small enough to operate in unique situations without a lot of material support or oversight. Large enough to rotate people on an as needed basis to keep from having them recognized. A group of volunteers who are already trained and ready to be deployed anywhere at any time with no more than twenty-four hours of notification."

Michael thought for a minute. "Okay, I like the idea but doesn't the military already have special units like what you're talking about?"

Sullivan nodded. "Yes Sir we do, but you don't."

"I don't understand, General."

"You have your Secret Service detail—keep them. What you don't have is a dedicated group that can operate where they need to be or whatever mission you send them on and only reports to you."

Michael shook his head. "Well, I like the idea but the Constitution does not permit the President his own secret, private bunch of head hunters. Besides, there's is no way to put something like that in the budget and keep it under wraps."

Sullivan smiled. "You wanna bet?"

Chapter Thirty-Seven

Harvey Bishop knocked on the door to Sullivan's private residential study. "Come on in, Harvey."

Bishop entered, walked to the desk and hit Parade Rest. Sullivan looked up. "Damnit Harvey... is there anyone else in the house?"

Bishop frowned. "Ah... no Sir."

"Then sit down Harvey... take a load off... RELAX!"

Bishop sat down on the chair in front of Sullivan's desk and waited until Sullivan had finished the report. "Well, we actually did pretty good, I think. As it stands, about a third have sent word that they won't be able to be part of the mission but appreciated the opportunity."

"We lost a third... already?" Bishop said in disbelief. "I just don't know what has gotten into all these young people. Ain't nothing like when you and I joined up, Sir."

"Harvey, when you joined up, our enemies were still shooting bows and arrows at us."

"Sir, that ain't nice," Bishop said, frowning. "I told you it hurts my feelings when you talk about how old I am."

"Harvey, Command Sergeant Majors are not supposed to have feelings. That's what you told me when I got you promoted and asked how you felt with the new chevron."

"Yeah, I did say that, didn't I? Anyway, how many more do you think we will lose?"

Sullivan shook his head. "Not enough to stop the plan; I figure that we can do what needs doing with eight, ten would be better. Anything over that is gravy."

"Everything set up for tomorrow morning?"

Bishop nodded. "I have all good-to-go, Sir."

Sullivan nodded and smiled. "Well, Harvey if we are GTG, take the rest of the day off. Relax."

Bishop looked at his watch. "Roger that, General. Appreciate the gesture but do you realize it's already 2130 hours?"

Sullivan glanced at his watch. "Well so it is, Sergeant Major..." Both finished the statement together, "Time sure flies when you're having fun," and laughed.

"Thanks Harvey," Sullivan said. Bishop stood and turned, waving over his shoulder.

Chapter Thirty-Eight

"Morning people," Sullivan said as he entered the hanger bay. Metal chair legs squealed on the concrete floor as the meeting attendees got up. Sullivan waved and said, "As you were, this isn't a formal gathering." He got to the front of the group and handed a file to Bishop. "Sergeant Major, would you call the roll please?"

Bishop opened the file and began reading names off in alphabetical order. "Here," "Yo," or "Here Sergeant Major," were the responses. Bishop closed the file, did a smart About Face, took two steps forward and handed the file to Sullivan. "All present or accounted for, Sir."

"Thank you Sergeant Major and thank each of you for coming," he said to the group gathered. "This will be the one and only meeting for some of you... this will be the first meeting of several for the rest of you. Today, I am going to give you some very broad parameters about why you're here and what I want you to do. Let me say right now, I am asking for volunteers." Groans came from the group. Sullivan laughed, "Damnit, I said I'm asking for volunteers not picking them."

The group laughed with him, government issue humor is seldom understood by civilians but it bands fighters together. "Some of you are not going to volunteer, I know that," Sullivan said. "Some of you have new lives, new families, new jobs... new girlfriends you can't leave." Catcalls followed by laughter filled the hanger. Sullivan smiled and thought, *God, I love these men and I miss them.*

"Seriously, as I said I know some of you can't join me. I just wanted each of you to know I thought enough of you to ask." Applause replaced the catcalls and laughter. Sullivan nodded. "Sergeant Major, would you pass out the folders?" Bishop gathered the stacks of folders and carried them to the first row of chairs.

"Take one and pass the rest back." It didn't take long before each person had a file called "Unit 917." Sullivan stood up. "Now, I want you to read these folders and talk among yourselves. We will reconvene in two hours for questions. You are free to ask any question you wish. I on the other hand may not be able to answer your question at this time for security reasons. I will do my best and, when you leave here today, you will have as much information as I can give you. For the next five days talk among yourselves... think it over and when we meet again, you will give me your answer. Are you in or not? Until then you are my guests.

"Those who choose for whatever reason not to join in may do so freely, and without prejudice or negative feelings. Those of you who decide you will join will have an additional two weeks to return to your homes and make arrangements for an extended leave from your normal lives."

"How long, General?" Someone hollered from the back of the room.

Sullivan smiled but did not answer. "We will reconvene in here at..." he checked his wrist watch, "at 1145 hours." Sullivan turned and walked to the exit with Sergeant Major Bishop on his heels. Members of the group looked from side-to-side trying to figure out what they should do next... they had never seen a formation like this one.

Finally, the guy who had asked "How long" stood up. "Okay, guess this is where we break up into groups. I suggest you, you and you," pointing to the older guys, "pick places in the hanger for us to meet in groups. I'm not real sure what the hell we're doing here but we only have two hours to decide what questions to ask. Let's get at it."

The group broke into small sections that drifted to different parts of the hanger. From time to time, one or several group members would migrate to other groups for their opinions and questions. The two hours went by rather quickly.

Chapter Thirty-Nine

Dr. David Blackman, Chief of Psychological Research at Mid-Wake, was making his rounds when his message beeper went off. He recognized the number and the *** following it. *Hmmm, wonder what the emergency is*, he thought, realizing he had left his cell phone in its charging cradle. He stopped at the nurse's station and reaching over the counter said, "Hello Nurse Adkins, may I borrow your phone?"

"Certainly, Doctor," Nurse Adkins said, setting the telephone on the raised counter in front of her computer. Blackman got an outside line and dialed the number. "Dr. Blackman returning a call…"

"One moment, Doctor…" the secretary said and "mood" music sounded in his ear.

"Sullivan."

"David Blackman, returning your call, General."

"Yes, yes… Doctor, I need to see you. Are you at Mid-Wake?"

"No Sir. As a matter of fact I'm making rounds at the Psych Unit at Honolulu General this morning."

"Keeping up with patient care, I see," Sullivan barked with a snort of humor. "Doc, I need to see you as soon as possible. I'm sending a car for you, hate to mess up your day but this is an emergency."

"I'm at your disposal General. Can you tell me what this is about?"

"Not on the phone, Doc. Be ready, the car will meet you at the front entrance in…" Sullivan checked his desk clock. "In twenty minutes to bring you to my office. Please be ready," Sullivan said, breaking the connection without waiting for an answer. Blackman frowned and began dialing another hospital extension.

"Dr. Jennings, this is Dr. Blackman. Can you pull the rest of my rounds, I have an emergency." Jennings agreed and Blackman told him to check with Nurse Adkins at the Fifth floor nurse's station for the charts and hurried to the Doctor's lounge to change his white jacket for his suit coat.

*****

"Thanks for coming, Doc," General Sullivan said as Dr. Blackman entered his office. Stepping around his desk, Sullivan shook hands with Blackman and grabbed his saucer hat from the coat rack. "Follow me, Doc. We can talk on the way." Sullivan led the way out his private entrance and down the stairwell.

"Where are we going, General?"

"Over to Building C, Doc," Sullivan said without explanation. "Want to pick your brain a little."

"What about?"

"You'll see, Doc," Sullivan said as they exited his building and started across the complex to Building C. Sullivan's pace was like a quick step march and Blackman had to hurry his steps to keep up with him. They entered Building C and headed to the second floor. As they approached the Entry Control Point the guard, a senior NCO snapped to attention. "Afternoon Sir."

"Hello, Sergeant," Sullivan said as he signed in on the controlled entry form. Blackman flashed his identification card and signed in also. The guard examined their signatures, checking Blackman's against the ID card signature and hit a hidden button allowing the electronic lock to disengage on the door behind him.

"Thank you, Gentlemen," he said as he opened the door for the two men.

"Thanks Son," Sullivan said taking Blackman's arm. "Come on Doc," Sullivan said, stepping off, down the hall with Blackman rushing to keep up. They entered the last office on the left side of the hallway and Blackman followed Sullivan through the anteroom and into a secure interrogation room. Sitting at the table was a well dressed, immaculate older gentleman with long white hair and white beard. "Doctor, I believe you are acquainted with The Keeper?"

"Yes, I am. How are you, Sir?" Blackman said, smiling.

The Keeper stood and extended his hand. "I am well Doctor, it is good to see you again, even under these circumstances."

Blackman shook the proffered hand and sat down. "Unfortunately, Sir, the General has not briefed me yet on the circumstances." He turned to Sullivan and cocked an eyebrow in question.

Sullivan pulled a chair from under the table, spun it around, and sat down, using the back of the chair as an armrest. "This room is screened to prevent all electronic intrusion or surveillance. It is swept twice daily routinely and prior to each use during the day. We can speak freely. Doc, what do you know about telepathy?"

Blackman looked up at the ceiling for a moment as his mind raced to locate an old memory file. He began reciting from memory, "Telepathy is part of what many refer to as extrasensory perception or ESP. Simply, it is normally construed as mind-to-mind communication between two or more people. It has been described as getting someone else to think or feel or hear something from another person, usually at some distance, without direct physical contact.

"No sounds or symbols are used; nothing, in fact, except pure thoughts sent from one person—the transmitter, to another person—the receiver."

The Keeper smiled. "Very good. Doctor, do you believe in telepathy?"

Blackman turned slightly to face the older man. "There was a lot of scientific study of ESP prior to the Night of the War and many of those records survived. While there were some interesting studies, nothing of great significance was presented. Most results could be described as anecdotal rather than factual and reproducible in a scientific experiment."

"What about your personal opinion?" The Keeper asked.

"Do I believe in ESP? Yes, yes I do. However, I do not believe in it the way it is normally portrayed in science fiction. I believe there are people who have greater or lesser degrees of extrasensory perception than the rest of us. That can include telepathy, psychokinesis, precognition and other psychic abilities.

"Telepathy itself is usually thought to mean planting a message, image or word into another person's mind. That is referred to as 'telepathic impression.' Mind reading, what most of us think about when considering telepathy, is sensing or copying but not interfering with what goes on in another's mind. Mind

102

control, actually commanding or compelling the thoughts and actions of an-other... Well, let me say there is a plethora of considerations there. Mental communication, well that is like using the mind as a wireless phone or radio without a monthly bill for services.

"Do I believe in it, yes, and so do a lot of others. Or at least they would like to. Studies show that when people are asked what 'super power' they would like to have, the two predominate answers are the ability to fly and mind control." Blackman smiled with a memory. "One of my professors, a fine older gentlemen with a devoted spiritual nature, once told me something. He said, 'If telepathy is real, I think God turned it off for our own good.' I have seen studies to promote the probability, not just a possibility, of interspecies communications. Like pet owners and their pets seem to 'know' each other."

The Keeper turned to Sullivan. "General, I believe it is possible to begin now."

Chapter Forty

Sullivan snorted. "Okay Doctor... I don't understand a lot of this mumbo jumbo; however, I am smart enough to know what I don't know. Here's the deal, The Keeper has been in mental contact with John Rourke several times. What you called 'mental communication,' we need to establish that contact again.

"Secondarily." Sullivan stopped and pulled a single sheet of paper from his inside coat pocket and slid it across the table to Blackman. "Read it, sign it. Standard non-disclosure agreement, you've done them before."

Blackman gave a quick read then scrawled his signature at the bottom of the form and slid it back to Sullivan. "Secondarily? You were about to say..."

"Secondarily, I need you and The Keeper to attempt to access the memories of some individuals from the 442nd."

Blackman blinked. "You're talking about the clones?" Sullivan nodded. "We conducted a standard battery of tests on them after the tattoos were removed. I saw nothing that would suggest any of them had any higher or lower propensity for ESP than the average public."

Sullivan nodded. "I understand but as you said your tests were standard. I'm not talking about anything that you could call standard."

"Let me explain," said The Keeper. "Some, but not all of my people retain the ability to have 'mental communication' as you call it. It is said that long ago, all of my people had it and used it. Now there are only a few." The Keeper leaned forward. "Would you like for me to demonstrate it for you, Doctor?"

Blackman pulled back. "I... I don't know. What is involved?"

The Keeper reached across the table with both hands. "If you are willing, start by placing both of your hands in mine. Should the contact become unpleasant or unwanted or threatening in any manner, simply remove your hands from mine and the contact will be broken. It is essential that both parties are comfortable and trusting with the touching of minds."

Blackman held out his hands but did not grasp those of The Keeper; he turned and looked at Sullivan with a furrowed brow. Sullivan smiled. "It is up to you, Doc. I did it this morning with him. Don't understand a damn thing about it, but it is true." Blackman looked back at The Keeper.

The old man smiled a gentle smile and said, "I promise I will not bite." Blackman smiled back and settled his hands into those of The Keeper.

Chapter Forty-One

Blackman felt a tingle go through his body like electricity and then he felt a gentle probe in his mind. He shook his head to clear it but the probe again tickled his awareness. He stared into the eyes of The Keeper.

Then, barely a whisper at first, less than an impression, more like a mental breeze, a thought began to form in his mind. *Yes Doctor, it is me, Try to sit back and close your eyes.* Blackman shook his head again. *Trust me Doctor, please sit back and close your eyes, the first contact is always the most difficult.*

Blackman did not understand what was happening to him; was he finally losing his mind? The answer came unbidden to him. *No Doctor, you are fine. Just relax so I can reach you.*

Blackman spoke, "Keeper, is that you? What is happening?"

Yes Doctor, The Keeper smiled and closed his eyes. Blackman took the hint and allowed his eyes to close. *As I said Doctor, it is a gift some of my people have, seldom is it practiced anymore; it became unnecessary due to our close quarters during our journey. It is only practiced today by a certain few of my people. I look forward to more discussions with you in the future; I hope you will allow it.*

"Yes," Blackman said. "I will allow it."

It is better Doctor, if you do not speak aloud. Simply think what you want to say, speaking aloud makes our connection difficult. It is like you are shouting at me.

Blackman concentrated and thought, *I'm sorry, is this better?*

Yes, Doctor, do see how simple it is?

Blackman smiled. *Yes, this is incredible. Can you read my mind also?*

No Doctor, that would be invasive and unethical. Once I have established the link, we just talk to each other. I promise your thoughts are your own. When I attempt contact with another's mind, that person must be willing to accept the contact for us to communicate. It is not possible for either of us to pry into the other's thoughts. It is only possible to visit as we are doing.

Sullivan watched as Blackman nodded. Blackman thought, *I see. I think I understand.*

*****

When The Keeper broke physical contact with Blackman, Blackman did not move for several moments. Slowly he opened his eyes, blinked and looked around the room, then smiled. "That was incredible, unbelievable." He turned to The Keeper. "Thank you."

The old man smiled. "You are welcome, Doctor. How do you feel?"

"Dreamy, like I'm just waking up from a good night's sleep."

"That is good, thank you for trusting me," The Keeper said, smiling.

Blackman stretched and turned to Sullivan, "Okay, General… talk to me about the 'Secondarily' again."

Sullivan sat down. "Here's the deal, Doc. Recently, General Thorne was in the UFO we captured when he was engaged by two craft."

"Engaged, do you mean attacked?"

Sullivan nodded. "Yes."

"Is he alright?"

Sullivan nodded again. "Yes, and not only did Thorne survive, he destroyed both of his attackers."

"He was attacked by the Aliens and survived?"

"No Doctor, he was attacked by my people," The Keeper interjected.

"Your people, I thought the KI were friendly," Blackman said, incredulously.

Sullivan snorted. "So did we Doc, but apparently that bastard Captain of theirs has aligned himself with the Russians. Together they have modified some of the smaller KI craft into fighters that can operate both in the atmosphere and outside of it."

"I suspect," The Keeper said, "the main reason General Thorne survived, taking nothing away from his piloting skills… the main reason he won, was the inexperience of his opponents. Whether they KI or Russians, they did not have as much experience piloting those craft as they thought. Or at least not piloting them in a combat situation."

Blackman frowned. "General, you mentioned trying to tap into the minds of those cloned individuals who we rescued and are now in the service of our forces."

Sullivan nodded. "It is my theory… and only a theory… Once we removed those damn tattoos, contact with the Aliens was broken. However, when the attack came on the President's day of inauguration, there were several other craft that were shot down. Additionally, the clone forces were already located within the Waiāhole Ditch and Tunnel complex; quite a few of them I might add. Think about it, Doc. What does that suggest to you?"

Blackman was silent for almost a minute. "It suggests to me that A, the Aliens had more than the one craft we recovered. B, it is possible that some, if not all, of our rescued cloned individuals have flown or know how to fly those craft." Blackman thought for another minute, "It also suggests that General Thorne's fortune may not last long. The KI and Russians can build or modify more craft and train more pilots, but we only have one UFO and one trained pilot."

Sullivan slammed his hand down on the table top. "Exactly Doctor. Now you have a pretty clear view of my 'Secondarily,' don't you?"

Chapter Forty-Two

On board the lead ship in the KI Armada, the individual known as the Captain paced in his room. "How did this happen?" he said aloud to the empty room. "This is impossible; the Humans do not have the technology to defeat our technology." A trill sounded and the Captain turned to face the door to his quarters. "Enter."

"Zdravstvujtye, Captain," the Russian Spetsnaz Colonel said using the formal greeting.

The Captain smiled, he liked this game. "Dobroye utro!" This was the less formal greeting used before noon.

"Very good," the Colonel said with a smile. "Your Russian is improved."

The Captain walked over and extended his hand in greeting; he hated this custom but knew the Humans expected it. "My Russian is improving but my circumstances have not, Colonel."

Without being asked, the Colonel sat down in a chair. It was all The Captain could do to refrain from grabbing the man and physically throwing him through the bulkhead. Instead, The Captain took a seat behind his desk. "Explain to me why both of our craft were destroyed by the Humans."

"Frankly... I have no idea," the Russian said. "I know of nothing in the land, sea or air based arsenals of any government down there capable of destroying those craft. Either there was a catastrophic malfunction of one or both of the craft, some incredible pilot error, or... we have another player in the game."

The Captain frowned. "You are alluding to the Alien race my people dealt with so long ago?" The Colonel nodded. "But you told me your government had not dealt with them since before... what was that phrase... Aah, The Night of the War."

"That is correct, Captain. However, intelligence has determined that the Alien race has made contact with the Rourkes, albeit those contacts have been in the way of Alien produced Clones attacking them. There is also the 'unfortunate' reality that John Rourke remains missing. Our operatives have verified, from multiple sources, that he went missing during a 'supposed archaeological' mission to Mount Rushmore. In spite of our best efforts... we have no idea where he is being held or by who."

"What is that thing you told me the other day about the razor blade?"

The Colonel smiled. "Not razor blade my friend. It is called Occam's razor, a problem-solving principle attributed to an old English friar and scholastic philosopher and theologian. The principle can be interpreted as stating, 'Among competing hypotheses, the one with the fewest assumptions should be selected.'

"Another way of saying the simplest answer is usually the correct answer. In other words, we know for sure of three players in this game, the Humans, the KI and the Alien/Clones, who have attacked the Rourkes before. If we, the Humans, don't have Rourke... and you, the KI, don't have Rourke, the Aliens must have him."

"Likewise, if you did not destroy your own fighter craft and if we Humans have no way of destroying them..."

The Captain nodded. "The Aliens must have."

The Colonel smiled. "From the variables presented, that IS the most logical, and ergo, the most probable answer. Don't you agree?"

Chapter Forty-Three

Dr. David Blackman closed the file and leaned back in his chair. "Whew," he said standing and walking to the coffee pot for a cup. "Damn, did I drink it all?" Glancing at his watch he was stunned. "Hmmm, guess I did."

He walked to the office window and opened the blinds and blinked from the sting of the sunlight streaming in. He stretched and yawned. "Yeah… guess that was a longer night than I thought," he said to himself as he secured the file, locked the desk drawer it was in and headed down the hall to the restroom. He spotted Frank Sullivan coming toward him.

"Morning General."

"Morning hell, it's damn near noon," Sullivan said.

"Yeah, well for me its morning," Blackman said with a smile. "I haven't been to bed yet," he said as he pushed open the restroom door, Sullivan following him in.

Sullivan checked the two stalls and satisfied they were alone turned back to Blackman. "What did you find out, Doc?"

"First of all, I found out I'm getting too old for these all nighters," then said "Aaaah" as his bladder released and a stream of urine hit the bowl of the urinal. "Second, I found out my bladder is still functional and thirdly I found out we have six candidates from the 442nd for your experiment."

"Damn, I was hoping for more, their 'parents' were astronauts for Pete's sake."

Blackman agreed. "I was surprised a little myself but each of the Eden Project craft carried only one primary pilot, a backup pilot and a flight engineer who could take over in a pinch. The rest of the crew were all medical or scientific personnel. That gave us a potential group of fifteen." Blackman zipped his pants and stepped to the sink and washed his hands. Grabbing a paper towel, he said, "Seven of them were injured or killed in the attack at the Tunnel complex and two are unaccounted for. What is your next step?"

"Contact Akiro Kuriname and get them back to Honolulu so you and The Keeper can start working with them. How good are you at hypnosis, Doc?"

Blackman turned, stared at Sullivan and said in a Dracula voice, "Loook into my eyyes!"

Sullivan opened the door for Blackman and said, "Screw ya, Doc. I ain't lettin' you into my head."

"So, how do we proceed?" Blackman asked.

"Without you and The Keeper, we couldn't," Sullivan said. "We have trained specific members of the 442nd for a special mission. We went through the records of the old Eden Project to find those members who had actual flight experience before the Eden Project mission. It is our supposition that those individuals had muscle memory and a 'proclivity' for flight which may have been replicated in their clones."

"That makes sense," Blackman said, nodding.

"When they arrive," Sullivan continued, "I want you and The Keeper to find out if they have any 'lost' or 'hidden' memories of their time with the Aliens that might assist us."

"And if they do, you want us to tap into them and find out what they are? What then?"

Sullivan shrugged. "Not sure, won't be until you find out. There are three things I hope you can find out. First, do the Aliens in fact have more of these UFOs? Second, do we in fact have individuals that at one time knew how to fly them?"

Blackman nodded. "And if they did know how, it wouldn't be a great stretch for Thorne to remind them how to fly them."

Sullivan nodded. "Exactly."

"And the third thing?" Blackman asked, smiling.

Sullivan grew stern. "I want you to find out where the damned UFOs are at because I'll bet beans to bullets that's where John Thomas Rourke is."

Chapter Forty-Four

Kuriname and five of the 442nd walked down the cargo ramp of the VTOL transport and across the tarmac at the Kaneohe Marine Air Base toward two waiting vans. A Sergeant saluted and said, "Captain, if you and your men will dump your gear in the second van we'll get the weapons turned in and your duffels to your bunks."

"Thanks, Sergeant," Kuriname said returning the salute. "Any idea why we were recalled?"

The Sergeant shook his head as he grabbed Kuriname's duffle bag and walked to the second van. "Hell Sir, you know they don't tell us grunts anything except where to be and what to do when we get there." Five minutes later the two vans were both loaded and driven off in different directions. Fifteen minutes later, the one with Kuriname and his men pulled up to the Ambrose Federal Detention Center rear equipment entrance and unloaded.

Another NCO was waiting and escorted the six men through a maze of corridors and hallways, finally stopping at a small conference room where he held the door open. "In here gentlemen, I'll let them know you're here."

The team entered but before Kuriname could question the NCO, he had closed the door and was gone. Kuriname turned back to his people and said, "Take a seat guys, I'm sure we will find out what this is about shortly. Looks like they have a coffee pot and some donuts for us."

Ben Nehen smiled and said, "Hope they're not trying to fatten us up for the kill."

Several laughed but Akiro Kuriname was not one of them.

*****

The door opened and one of the 442nd hollered, "'Ten hut!"

"As you were," Sullivan said and walked directly to Kuriname. "Captain, how are you?"

"Sir," Kuriname said, accepting Sullivan's out-stretched hand, "a little confused to be honest with you. Can you tell me what this is all about?"

Sullivan turned back to the others. "Gentlemen, I'm sorry for the theatrics but we have a problem that only you can help with." The door opened again and Dr. Blackman and The Keeper entered. Sullivan introduced them.

Kuriname introduced his folks. "This is Commander Landon Billingsly, he was backup pilot and Lieutenant Layne Washington, Flight Engineer—both from Eden Three. Lieutenant Commander Charlie Carlton, backup pilot and flight engineer Lieutenant Frank Hayden, Eden Four and this is Lieutenant Mason Johnson. He was on Eden Two."

"Let's all take a seat, got a story for you," Sullivan instructed. After explaining what had happened on Thorne's flight with the attack by the KI fighters, Sullivan was silent.

Carlton was the first to speak. "General... what exactly does that have to do with us?"

"We think it is EXTREMELY likely the faction of the KI that launched the fighters either have more or will shortly," Sullivan said. "Currently, we only have one person, General Thorne, who is qualified to fly his craft, and the real bad part is we only have one of those craft."

Carlton said. "Again, Sir, what does that have to do with us?"

Sullivan took a sip of coffee and smiled, saying, "Don't know that it does Lieutenant Commander, but you guys are our best hope. Dr. Blackman, why don't you explain our theory?"

Fifteen minutes later, Akiro Kuriname raised his hand. "General, I cannot speak for anyone else but I'm not sure this will work. Honestly, I don't have what I would call 'memories' before I woke up after the surgery removing the tattoo. Just vague impressions..." He looked around the table and the other five were nodding.

"Seems like that's the case for all of us," Carlton said.

"The vague impressions tell us that something registered at some level chemically in your brains," Blackman said, smiling. "That also means those impressions might be able to be accessed with some gentle probing."

"I don't want anyone operating on my brain, Dr. Blackman," Johnson said.

The Keeper had remained quiet until now. He smiled, saying, "Not that kind of probing, I assure you Lieutenant Johnson."

"Here's how we think it will work; if you are willing," Blackman began. "I will attempt to put you in a relaxed hypnotic state. If that is successful, The Keeper will attempt to make contact with your mind and see if the 'vague impressions' can be developed into full-fledged memories. If so, that could be extremely helpful with planning how and what to do to meet this current threat. You will not be sedated or drugged in any form."

"What if it doesn't work?" Johnson asked.

"No guarantees it will," Sullivan said. "Some folks, for whatever reason, cannot be hypnotized. We can't say for sure. The Keeper will be able to make contact with that realm of your mind. Frankly however… we don't have any other options." The members of the 442nd sat quietly.

Kuriname stood. "I'll do it. I want to go first. If it works, let me explain it to my men and let them make up their own minds about it."

Chapter Forty-Five

Akiro Kuriname walked into Dr. Blackman's office. Nervously he asked, "Do you want me in the chair or on the couch?"

Blackman smiled. "Wherever you are most comfortable, Captain."

Kuriname chose the chair and sat down. Blackman fiddled with the rheostat light switch dimming the lights. "Have you ever been hypnotized, Captain?"

"I have not, to my memory; I cannot speak for my parent."

"Well, Akiro, may I call you Akiro?" Blackman said, his voice going soft and just to the left of monotonous.

"You may, Doctor."

Blackman smiled and sat in a chair next to Kuriname. "Call me David. Are you comfortable?" Kuriname nodded. "Here's is what is going to happen. We are going to simply chat for a while and I want you to relax. Gradually I want to guide you toward a state of complete ease and relaxation. I will try to deepen that state by suggestions which will allow your body to grow very, very still and quiet while your mind grows more and more focused, eventually entering the state we call somnambulism of hypnosis.

"In that state you will be so relaxed, you will forget your body and where you are, and you're just in a little world where I will use imagery or suggestions to guide your mind. When it's time to come back, I will guide you through a gradual process that allows your mind and body to reintegrate. You will become more and more alert and upon command, you will open your eyes and be fully conscious, relaxed and comfortable with no ill effects whatsoever."

Akiro nodded his understanding.

"Now," Blackman continued, "this first session many take a little longer than the others. I like to invite the client in and get to know her or him a little bit, establish a personal relationship. We have already done that. Then I explain how hypnosis works and why it works the way it does and what to expect. That's what I'm doing now."

Akiro could already feel himself relaxing, aware of how easy it was to listen to Blackman. His muscles seemed to have a will of their own as the tenseness left his body.

"I like to gradually introduce them to the concept of entering hypnosis. It should be as easy and painless as possible. Don't you agree, Akiro?" Kuriname only smiled a little. "That is very good, Akiro, would you close your eyes for me now?" Kuriname did and less than ten minutes later, Akiro Kuriname was in deep hypnosis and answering questions. Blackman flicked a switch under his desk and in an adjoining room a light went on. The Keeper stood up and quietly opened the private door behind Blackman's desk and entered the room.

He stood behind Kuriname and reached into the recesses of that mind with his own. Kuriname began to speak, answering silent questions The Keeper placed into his mind. Blackman took notes, capturing every answer; making notes of any physical reaction Kuriname had. The process continued for just less than two hours.

*****

After awakening, Kuriname was relaxed and well rested. He was comfortable with describing the process to the other five subjects. After a few moments of discussion they also agreed to the process.

Chapter Forty-Six

Michael Rourke and his Chief of Staff, General Frank Sullivan, looked up as Michael's Marine Guard knocked on the door and opened it. "They are here, Sir."

Michael nodded. "Send them in, Sergeant."

The Guard stepped back, saying, "Gentlemen." He held to door for the small parade to enter. Jose Zima, Steven Delervello, and Dr. David Blackman entered, followed by The Keeper. Zima was dressed in business casual as was his style; Delervello and Blackman were in dark suits. The Keeper looked like a character from a British tabloid of the late 1800s, in a tweed suit and Deer-stalker cap.

Michael looked at Sullivan who could not keep a slight grin from cracking his lips. "Keeper," Michael said. "That is a most striking outfit."

"Yes," The Keeper said. "I quite like it myself, it is tweed you know." Michael nodded and Sullivan looked down to hide his broadening grin. "My studies of your different styles tell me that tweed emerged in what was called Scotland and Ireland as a way for the farmers there to battle the chilly, damp climate which characterizes those parts."

Turning to show off his outfit, he said, "Tweed began as a hand woven fabric, rough, thick, and felted with colors muted and earthy. It was truly a working man's cloth, I rather like it. Some believe it was named for the River Tweed in Scotland, but a more popular legend says the name is a twist on the Scottish word for 'tweel' or twill. It is said that in 1826, a London clerk accidentally transcribed an order for 'tweel' and wrote 'tweed' instead, and from there the name came into use."

Sullivan swallowed hard to stifle a laugh. "I particularly like your cap, Sir."

The Keeper smiled, his long hair cascading out as he removed it. "Thank you, it is also tweed. Looks rather… dapper, is that the word?"

"It is close enough," Michael said. "Now, take a seat and tell me what you have learned."

Delervello started, "We have confirmed several things."

Dr. Blackman interrupted, "Yes, first of all... it was more difficult than we had thought but of the six men we interviewed, we were able to access deeply repressed memories of four that include operation of the Alien UFO craft. In separate interviews we have concluded that at the Alien complex, there are no less than five additional craft. Five that we are sure of."

"And it is possible there are more, possibly twice that many," Delervello said.

"And these four, they operated the craft at some time?" Michael asked.

"I believe so," Blackman said. "They appear to have operated the craft or had enough training that they were capable of operating them."

"My insight into those memories included images of them actually operating the craft along with sensations of physical interaction with the craft," The Keeper said. "Michael, there is something else also."

"What?"

"Memories of interactions between these men and the creature they called The Creator," The Keeper said.

"I would have expected that, provided you were able to access their memories," Michael said.

"Yes," said The Keeper, seriously. "But it was the content of those interactions."

"I don't understand."

The Keeper looked into Michael's eyes very intently before saying, "I fear we may have misjudged these creatures."

"Misjudged who, the Aliens?" Sullivan asked.

The Keeper nodded. "Yes, it is entirely possible that what we have surmised is nearly or very nearly... totally incorrect. I fear some of that is from information my people have given you. Of course, I won't know this for sure until I have had contact with The Creator myself."

Zima finally spoke. "Let me summarize for you, Mr. President. First of all, not only have four of the men either piloted or were trained to pilot the Alien craft, all six have been at the facility where the UFOs are kept. Secondarily, that facility is where the old rumors and General Thorne's flight describe it. Lastly, while there is no way to directly access the facility itself, there are ways in and out. The craft are located inside the facility and piloted outside via tunnels."

"Tunnels?" Sullivan asked loudly.

Zima nodded. "Tunnels, underground causeways, underground pathways, pipes… whatever you want to call them. The craft leave their bays within the pyramid and fly out and back through these tunnels. They exit the Earth approximately a half mile from the pyramid."

"There is one more thing," The Keeper said. "I accessed memories from each of these men concerning people… humans… who they encountered in the facility."

Michael frowned. "People from outside, not just other clones like themselves?"

The Keeper nodded. "Some apparently who had been there for some extended time periods; possibly decades."

Sullivan leaned back and boomed. "Doesn't sound to me like we misjudged them. Sounds like they have been abducting humans for God knows what kind of studies or analysis."

The Keeper shook his head. "I got the distinct feeling from the memories that these humans were well cared for. They were in good health and even 'valued.'"

Sullivan shook his head. "Valued? Slave owners valued their slaves. Mad scientists value their guinea pigs. Hunters value their trophies."

The Keeper nodded and said, "Yes, General, and parents value their children, teachers value their students and doctors value their patients. I do not know which of us is correct in our analysis; I will say we need to continue analyzing, however."

Chapter Forty-Seven

The next morning Sullivan walked into the doctor's office. "Well Doc, how is my boy?"

"Physically, he is fine, General," the doctor reported to Sullivan.

"Physically?" Sullivan frowned. "What about mentally?"

"Oh, I think he is fine there also," the doctor said. "But he is grouchy, argumentative…"

Sullivan nodded. "Can I see him doctor?"

"Yes General, but you may regret it," the doctor said as he opened the door.

"Morning Rodney," Sullivan smiled through the slightly opened door.

Thorne looked up, anger obvious on his face. He waved his hand around at the room and sullenly asked, "This your idea?"

"Yeah, sorry about that." Sullivan entered the room holding his hands up in surrender. "But I needed to be sure you were okay."

"Fine, I'm okay," Thorne snapped. "Now, can I get outta here?"

"After you tell me everything you can remember about the fighters who attacked you."

"Damnit, General," Thorne said exasperated. "I gave you the chip."

Sullivan drew himself up to his full height and set his jaw. "Let me tell you something One Star… you see these three stars? I out rank you Mister and your attitude right now needs to be adjusted. Am I clear?" Thorne started to say something but Sullivan cut him off, "Am I clear, BRIGADIER General Thorne?"

Thorne withered under Sullivan's glare and nodded, "You are, Lieutenant General. I apologize."

Sullivan thawed. "I know what's the matter with you Rodney. You're mad because those bastards jumped you and you never saw them coming, right?" Thorne nodded. Sullivan opened the door and waved his right hand for someone to come in. A female major in a Class A uniform, a Class A uniform that did nothing to hide the curves of her hips or the swell of her breasts, walked in carrying an old style Stenotype machine.

Thorne looked at Sullivan who winked. Sullivan said, "General Thorne this is Major Allison Evans, she will take your statement. Major Evans, General Rodney Thorne."

"Pleased to meet you, Major," Thorne said. "You are a stenographer? I was not aware that skill was still being used these days."

"Only in special circumstances, General." Major Evans smiled and continued to set up the Stenotype. "General Sullivan prefers them for special interviews where secrecy is of the highest importance."

Sullivan turned and walked out of the room with a big smile on his face. "He ain't gonna yell at her, I'll bet you."

Chapter Forty-Eight

Thorne got a clean bill of health and then he got the hell out of the hospital; almost. Three steps before he hit the main exit a voice called, "General Thorne." He turned, Frank Sullivan folded a newspaper he had hidden behind and stood up. *Damnit,* Thorne thought but smiled and said, "Hello, General. Good to see you again."

"Come on Rodney, I'll give you a lift."

"Thanks, Sir, but that's really not necessary."

Sullivan smiled. "Yeah… yeah it is. I've got to brief you. How are you doing?"

Damnit, Thorne thought but smiled and said, "Lead on, Sir. I'm fine; Doc gave me a Return to Duty Slip."

"Here's the deal, Rodney," Sullivan said once they were in his car. "I've got a mission for you. In fact, I have two."

Thorne buckled his seat belt. "Okay shoot."

Sullivan stomped the gas and his red touring car jumped forward; fifteen seconds later he was out of the parking lot and headed for the Main Gate. "You'll find out soon enough. Patience Rodney, patience."

Thorne looked out his side window for a second. Sullivan didn't elaborate and Thorne was smart enough not to press. *He'll tell me when he is ready, I guess.*

"Now," Sullivan asked. "How are you really?"

"Damnit," Thorne bellowed. "I told you, I'm alright." The outburst was not at all common for the normally unflappable pilot.

*****

For thirty minutes, neither spoke. Sullivan stopped along one of the beach front roads on the southeast side of the island. It was an area that didn't get much traffic. Sullivan engaged the parking brake; he reached in the console then looked at Thorne and said, "You coming?"

Thorne got out quickly and jogged forward to catch up with Sullivan. He saw three dark government sedans parked ahead of them. Sullivan motioned to the right and they headed down to the beach before reaching the sedans. A tall man stood staring out at the ocean; Thorne recognized him and thought, *Holy Crap!*

"Sir," Sullivan said over the pounding surf. Michael Rourke turned around. Thorne stopped in his tracks and saluted.

Michael smiled. "As you were General, this is a private conversation. Frank, did you bring 'em?" Thorne blanched then hesitantly dropped the salute.

Sullivan held up three dark cigars. "Sure did, even one for this guy." He handed one to Michael, gave one to Thorne, keeping one for himself. He peeled the wrapper and stuck out his hand to take the other two wrappers and stuck them in his pocket. He passed the cigar cutter and the lighter to Michael who puffed his cigar to life before passing it to Thorne. Thorne passed them back to Sullivan a little sheepishly.

Once all three cigars were lit, Michael looked at Thorne and said, "I need your help."

"What can I do, Mr. President?"

"For starters I need you to train some additional pilots to fly ships like yours, what do you call it… The Egg?" Thorne smiled and nodded. "Then I want you to lead an element in an operation to find my father, make contact with an Alien race I believe is holding him. If possible I want you to borrow as many ships like yours as they will let us have." Thorne's head was already spinning.

"Then I want you to personally lead an assault against a radical faction within the KI that have aligned with some rogue Russians." Michael drew on the cigar. Snapping his fingers, Michael added, "OH crap, almost forgot… I'll need you to help me with the Russians, too."

Thorne, who didn't normally smoke, was feeling a little green around the gills. "You said for starters… What else do you have in mind for me, Mr. President?"

"I also need you to provide air cover and cloaking for a team moving from a location in Georgia to one in Missouri. You'll get all of the details if you agree to my requests. I'll want you to coordinate what we have discussed with General Sullivan. What you are going to need, when you are going to need it and how much are you going to need. Once you have those details worked out and the two of you feel comfortable, let me know. Then we are going to have a meeting with some very select individuals. That meeting will form the basis for our actions, if the operation I mentioned actually succeeds."

Thorne nodded. "And if it doesn't succeed?"

Michael took a draw on his cigar and looked into Sullivan's eyes. He turned and tossed the cigar butt into the foam of the waves. "If it doesn't succeed Rodney... my father, the Rourke family and the world as we know it, will lose its fire just like that cigar did."

They walked the beach until they came to three large boulders and sat down. "All right gentlemen," Michael Rourke said. "The time has come for some hard decisions. Decisions you are going to have to make. As we speak, preparations are being made on a project designated as Fall Back. Paul Rubenstein and I—well actually, Paul has had the biggest part of it... was actually his idea... Anyway, Fall Back should be completed in the next three or four weeks."

Thorne raised his hand. "What exactly is Fall Back, Sir?"

"You have heard about the Retreat my father built?" Thorne nodded. "Well, Fall Back, this is the Retreat that Paul and I are constructing. Now here's the point... I am about to resign and when that happens our friends in the Progressive Party are coming after me and my family with a vengeance. My sources have penetrated their curtain of secrecy and luckily I know their plans. I also know who many of their covert operatives are and frankly fellas... the list would amaze you. Unfortunately, I don't know who all of them are and therein lies the problem."

Thorne sat up straighter. "Resign, you can't resign!"

Sullivan spoke, "Cool your jets, General. Listen to the man."

Michael cleared his throat. "The point is, the world has changed significantly from the time my father built the original Retreat. The threat has changed, the players have changed... Rodney, I cannot leave The Egg in the hands of people who would abuse it and use it against our country or my family. Nor can I afford to lose who currently is the only pilot."

Thorne stood facing out to sea for a long moment, finally, he spoke. "Mr. President... I have a family; a wife and four children. Permission to speak freely, Sir?" Michael nodded and Thorne looked away before turning back to Michael. "With what you're telling me we are about to abandon the country. And once that occurs, the forces I have stood against all of my life are going to take over, correct? Why the hell don't we stand and fight the bastards, Mr. President?"

"General Thorne, if for one moment I thought the process of standing and fighting would work—I would. The problem is, the country... its people have changed. In the past, Americans were fiercely independent, opinionated and strong. There was a sense of strength and pride in doing for ourselves. All Americans ever asked for was a chance, a chance to make it better for our kids than we parents had. A chance to make a positive difference. A chance to live free.

"That has been replaced in large part by an attitude of entitlement, a desire to be 'taken care of,' a commitment to nothing bigger than the individual or finer than 'just good enough to get by.' I don't know where it started or when it started or even who started it... but it is real and it is a poison more deadly to this country than the bombs that dropped on The Night of the War. We survived that... we can't survive this.

"The country has to move on its own to a renewed commitment to freedom, to the idea that the strength of the country is based on the strength of the individual, back to strength through diversity... back to the basics our Founding Fathers created this county on."

Thorne's eyes flared. "Damn it, Mr. President, I don't need a politician's election speech. I need the damn truth."

A light flashed in Michael's eyes and his right hand twitched, as if absently longing for the grip of his old .44 magnum. Standing very slowly and keeping his eyes locked on Thorne's, he walked slowly forward. "Rodney, let me tell you something, I lost my first wife, I have just lost my step-father and my half-brother, and I have no idea where my father is. Hell Rodney, I lost my whole damn world. I have fought this battle for so long; I started as a child and now I have children. And if there are any things I have learned in my life, here they are:

"First, winning can mean many things but the first thing it means is you have to survive long enough to win. I want you to understand that I am not speaking to you as your President. I am speaking man to man, father to father and husband to husband to you. I am taking my family with me to protect them. There is enough room for you to bring your family also. The second thing I have learned is if we don't have our families… what is the sense in surviving or winning?"

Michael turned to Sullivan and cocked an eyebrow. "What about you, Frank?"

"Hell Sir," Sullivan said. "I don't have a problem going with you. Wife's been dead for five years, we never had kids. This job never gave me the opportunity to build long lasting friendships… people kept dying on me and I just kept marching around them and going forward. I'm in."

Thorne stood, shaking his head. Michael asked, "Rodney, are you turning down my offer?"

Thorne looked up. "Huh, what? No, no Sir. I'm with you. I'm just trying to figure out how to tell my wife and kids about this."

Michael shook his head. "You can't… not yet. For right now this absolutely must stay between us. When the time is right I will let you know, and I'll even be there with you if you want me to be."

Chapter Forty Nine

Paul turned his back to the Arctic blast that threatened to knock him over while he stood alongside Akiro Kuriname and his Dog Soldiers as they unloaded equipment from the two VTOL planes on the shattered old runway. Kuriname, temporarily furloughed from his Egg pilot training program at Paul's request, ignored the wind and the cold. Focused on lining up the vehicles and equipment necessary for the next leg of this mission, he stood frowning into the wind.

In a strange twist of fate, the old Springfield-Branson Airport was in fact only a few miles, as the crow flies, from the entrance of the Caverns. AATVs—the old style armored all-terrain vehicles—with the old communications gear were off loaded from the VTOLs and the Dog Soldiers broke off into teams. Soon eight AATVs formed up into two arrowhead shaped formations and moved out across the frozen ground.

Between the two formations was a ninth vehicle; in it Paul Rubenstein and Randall Walls rode in the back passenger compartment. Walls was maintaining contact with the aerial command center. "Damn, it's cold," Walls said as he zipped the closure on his parka hood, leaving just his eyes and nose showing.

Rubenstein nodded. "Yes, but not as bad as I expected. We're about 150 miles north of the 35th parallel which is the glacial line. Honestly, I thought we would be on ice. I think this is another indication that the glaciers are receding as the weather warms. Truthfully if it wasn't for the wind, this wouldn't be too bad."

Walls looked out at the desolate landscape. "Yeah, not too bad at all."

Rubenstein was focused on the small screen on the instrument he held on his lap. The topographic map showed where the opening of the Fantastic Caverns used to be and the blinking pip showed the relationship between it and the AATVs as they closed the distance. Even though by line of sight it was only a few miles, on the surface there were repeated switchbacks and delays as the Dog Soldiers encountered huge cracks in the surface of the earth and sink holes the size of football fields. There were also landslides that had wiped out roads which once carried tourists to the Caverns.

Instead of the gentle rolling hills Paul remembered from so long ago, the terrain was stark and forbidding. Like a giant had grabbed the earth itself, ripping huge chunks and throwing them haphazardly. Paul knew that they would get to the GPS location, but the closer they came the worse the terrain was. He wondered if access could ever be gained to the Caverns, or were they lost to the world of man as they had been for eons prior to their discovery in the 1800s.

That is not an option as far as I am concerned, Paul thought. *Without the Caverns, I'm not sure the family can survive long enough to accomplish everything Michael and I have talked about.*

The cold had long ago permeated their Arctic clothing and Akiro Kuriname was about to call for a break when he felt a slap on his right shoulder and slowed the AATV, keying his microphone. He stopped the lead element ahead of them and pulled to a stop. He turned off the engine and turned around to speak to Paul. "Are you sure, Paul?" Akiro said without enthusiasm. "I don't see a damn thing."

Paul unbuckled and stepped out, relieved to be out of the bucking, jarring vehicle. It had taken a total of three and a half hours to go what would have been about three miles by air had there been a way to land the VTOLs any closer. Problem was the terrain—it was so broken, either caved in or there were great sections of rock shoved up through the earth. Sometimes there had not been room for the AATVs to pass even in single file, which caused them to back track and search for a clear pathway.

"We're there," Paul said looking at the screen as a set of numbers blinked: 37.2874° N, 93.3585° W. He walked to the edge of a cliff. Below, several hundred feet below and several hundred feet to the left, Paul thought he could hear the rush of water. Could it be?

Paul went back to the AATV and pulled a map from his case. "Yes, it has to be…" Paul said aloud to himself.

"Has to be what?" Akiro asked.

Paul smiled. "The Little Sac River ran along the northeast side of the Caverns. What we're hearing must be its waters still flowing after all this time. Akiro, we need to get down there." Paul pointed over the edge of the cliff.

"We'll have to do it in stages," Akiro said finally. "We don't have enough repelling rope to make it in one jump. Plus," he said, looking into the gorge below, "I don't know how but there is a lot, and I mean a lot, of foliage that starts about a quarter of the way down. It is older stuff, trees as well as undergrowth. There must be a heat vent somewhere in the gorge. The foliage is thick and it is going to be hard to hack through but we have to. That stuff is way too thick to even try and land one of the VTOLS without preparing an LZ."

Akiro turned to Charlie Whitehorse and shouted, "Take three troopers and rig up the ropes! I want you to establish an overwatch right here on the lip of the drop off; half of your people covering the folks going down and half watching behind us."

Kuriname turned to another of his Native American Dog Soldiers, Benjamin Nehen. "Ben, I want you to take two AATVS and find a way to drive to the bottom of this gorge. You're probably going to have to go several miles southwest to find a path... if there even is one." Pointing to the communication specialist, he added, "Check in every thirty minutes with Travis here so we know about where you are and that you're okay. Set up your other AATVs and men here with Whitehorse's men for cover. Mr. Walls, I want you to stay up here with my men."

Walls nodded. "Paul, you going over the cliff?"

Paul pushed his glasses further up on his nose, grabbed a small day pack and put it on. Slinging the Schmeisser across his back, over the day pack and letting it hang by his left hand, Paul nodded and smiled. He checked the strap holding the High Power in the shoulder holster under his left arm. "Yup, ain't nothin' to it, Randall. Just like jumpin' off a tall building in a single bound."

Walls smiled. "Better you than me, just watch out for Kryptonite and jerks trying to kill you."

Two men, with coils of additional rope slung over one shoulder, went over the edge on two separate ropes. Unlike in practice, there was no one to belay them. If they fell, they fell and almost certainly would die.

Shortly, two more descended and then it was Paul's turn. He snagged the rope and handed his Figure-8 descender to one of the Dog Soldiers who was serving as a safety man. The man looped the rope through and around the neck of the descender then turned it over and snapped it into the harness Rubenstein wore. Taking the long end of the rope, what repellers referred to as "the bitter end," in what Paul assumed was some kind of graveyard humor. He moved back to the edge.

The wind was too strong to be heard so instead of yelling "On Repel" he raised one gloved hand and clenched his fist. The man below, the third to go down the cliff face, signaled back that he was "On belay." With his right foot Paul stepped over the ledge, and in another step was "standing" with his feet against the cliff face with several hundred feet of empty space below him. With short controlled jumps during which the rope slid rapidly through the glove on his right hand, Paul descended. The right hand was the "break hand" and by squeezing his fist and pulling the rope to his side, Paul controlled the rate he descended.

The left hand was used simply as a guide. He kept it above the Figure 8 and loose on the rope. If need be he could "lock up" his descent and return fire with the Schmeisser using his guide hand. So far, that had not been necessary; it seemed the area was devoid of life except for in the gorge. Paul watched the tree tops below him get closer and then he was on a ledge with his belay man. He unhooked from the rope he had come down on and hooked onto another rope that had been rigged to the rock face for the next step of his descent.

When the last man came down from the top he would unhook the rope, thread it back through the piton and go down half the distance of a full length of rope. He would pull the rope free, set another piton, hook up and begin the next phase of the drop. Finally, an hour and fifteen minutes after starting, all of the men stood on the floor of the gorge.

Paul did the math and determined the cliff face was over 650 feet high. Kuriname had been right, there had to be a heat vent down there. Men were already removing their Arctic parka and extreme cold weather pants. Kuriname came up to help Paul remove his gear. "It must be at least twenty, maybe thirty degrees warmer down there."

Paul nodded. "Yeah, and the wind does not appear to be able to penetrate into the gorge."

Kuriname formed up his men in two squads, one going left and the other right, searching for something that could be the opening. "Do you think we can find a way in Paul?"

Paul shrugged as he walked with Akiro. "Honestly, I did. Now, seeing this... I just don't know. None of the satellite images showed this much topographic damage. I just don't know. Have you heard anything from Ben's team?"

"Nehen checked in about ten minutes ago. He thinks they have found a pathway. They are pushing toward us now." And so the search began...

Chapter Fifty

Sergeant Major Bishop handed the final list to Sullivan. "So Harvey, these are the volunteers?"

"Yes, Sir. We had four more but they didn't pass the physical," Bishop said. "You told me not to fudge on any of them, right?"

"Absolutely not," Sullivan said. "Their primary functions will be to accomplish these missions and safeguard the President in the field. They have to be the best of the best or this won't work. I'm glad we have so much medical experience on the team; that alone makes me feel better."

Bishop nodded. "I think for a team made up purely on 'luck of the draw,' it is pretty balanced." Bishop noticed Sullivan was frowning, "What's the matter, General?"

"Trying to think of a name, Harvey. We have to call 'em something, you know."

"Relax Sir, got that worked out. The unit radio call sign will be 'Papa-Papa,' numerical adjustments like 'Papa-Papa One' or 'Two' you can assign."

"And Papa-Papa stands for what, Harvey?" Sullivan asked with trepidation.

"Why that's simple Sir, POTUS POSSE. Per your instructions, General... the Posse will be listed as 'private contractors and consultants.' They will be paid out of the General Appropriations Fund set up by the President for wildlife monitoring and conservation."

Sullivan smiled. "Excellent Sergeant Major, that will work."

Chapter Fifty-One

The search had gone on for over two hours with no luck. Paul checked his watch, it was time. He radioed Akiro Kuriname. "Search One, this is Handler, over."

"Go ahead Handler. Over."

"It's time to put them up. Over."

"Handler, this is Search One, we still haven't got anything. Over."

"Search One, it doesn't matter. Put out the units and activate. We will have to adjust the coverage as the search continues. Over."

"Roger that, Handler," Kuriname said. "Give us fifteen minutes. Over."

"You have ten minutes, Search One, and not a minute more. Over." It took only eight. Two minutes, thirty seconds later, one of the camera satellites was set to pass over the area. Even though it belonged to America, it could not be allowed to see the area uncloaked.

Camouflage has been part of winning battles and often avoiding them since the first time one group decided to attack another group. When trying to disguise a fixed position, like a cave entrance, there are several methods of camouflage. Hiding the operational aspects of getting into and out of the cave is one thing; hiding the mechanisms is important. John had used weights and counter balance technology in the Georgia Retreat, similar to what had been used in the Egyptian pyramids and Mayan Temples of Central America.

Rubenstein saw no sense in developing other techniques; after all, Rourke had taught him, "If it ain't broke, it ain't broke."

Another issue was once the entrance and the entry mechanism were hidden, they'd have to hide the visible parts of the structure itself. Colors and texture is as important as the concepts. Camouflage is most often colored with dull hues that match the predominant colors of the surrounding immediate area. In jungle warfare, camouflage is typically green and brown, to match the forest foliage and dirt. In the desert, a range of tan colors to match the sand and rocks. Whites and grays are used for snowy climates.

The texture is part of the visually disruptive process. A piece of mottled camouflage helps break the contour, the outline, of a structure or a person. The human brain naturally "connects the dots" and straight lines and shapes of manmade structures. To hide, you must affect the way you perceive and recognize the person or object wearing that camouflage.

That which cannot be buried out of sight must be dealt with by matching colors and patterns. The conscious human mind makes sense out of information, but the brain has to break it down into bits and pieces. If your brain perceives a long, vertical area of brown with green blotches connected to it, you perceive a tree. And when your brain perceives many, many individual trees in a given area, you perceive a forest.

Paul knew that detection systems were different and better than when John had created the original Retreat. He would also have to deal with thermal imaging that could see heat emitted by a person or piece of equipment. This did not even include radar, image enhancement and satellite photography and sophisticated listening devices.

Incorporated in this Retreat would be a way to keep excess heat from escaping and creating a thermal "signature" that would show up on a thermal imaging scan. For machinery, the major heat source is the engine exhaust. This could be defeated by passing the exhaust through ground water or another cooling system before it was released into the open air.

The main problem would be how to convert the original drive through cavern into a hidden and secure Retreat, capable of supporting a much larger contingency than its predecessor had dealt with.

Satellite photography was a major problem; Paul had to figure on a sophisticated smoke screen that could be implemented and kept in place until all modifications had been completed. Amazingly, he realized the Alien technology that had been captured at the Battle of the Forest and reverse engineered, solved his problem quite nicely.

The cave negated the need for stealth technology. Going underground meant radar absorbent material; dirt, in this case, covered the entire structure. The uneven surface eliminated flat planes that would reflect radio waves back for detections.

Now, he just needed to figure out how to get in…

Chapter Fifty-Two

Michael Rourke and Command Sergeant Major Bishop were watching the "Potus Posse" going through an exercise. Michael was impressed at the scope of the training. Not only was there the expected gunfire, but vehicle operation, communications… everything one would expect in the field was addressed.

There were even built-in scenarios where equipment failed and operations were interrupted by simulated injuries or just the 'fog of war' stuff that plagues real operations. After two hours Bishop escorted Michael to the team leader and introduced the man. "Sir, this is Ryan J. Fleming, Team Leader." Michael shook Fleming's hand, guessing the man stood over six and a half feet tall, probably closer to six-nine. He had piercing blue eyes; his dark blond hair was closely cropped in a military style haircut and spoke with what Michael thought sounded like a British accent.

He carried himself, and the Lancer Model M1A1 .308 rifle, with a casual confidence. Bandoliers of 20-round magazines criss-crossed over the torn and dirty t-shirt that covered his massive chest. Around his waist hung an antique .45 Model 1911, a large bowie knife and something that Michael recognized— a Lancer version of the old Ruger Redhawk .44 magnum. All three firearms looked used but well taken care of. Fleming was a shooter, that much was evident.

"Pleased to meet you, Sir. General Sullivan has spoken highly of you," Fleming said and launched into an animated conversation with Michael. Michael decided he liked the big man; he was funny but there was something that hinted he was a loner. It wasn't long before Michael also had him pegged as not only a sarcastic wise-ass, but a good leader. Even in polite conversation he thought Fleming could be described as a "sniper with his words," only speaking when it's something worth saying. Fleming seemed world-wise. Michael decided Fleming would not be easily fooled and preferred to go it alone whenever possible.

"You sure handled that exercise well," Michael said finally. "But tell me, how did a guy with a British accent get picked by General Sullivan for this special team?"

"Ah, yes, the General and I have worked together on several projects before his current position took him out of the field," was all Fleming said. Michael found a complexity to the big man and thought, *As big as he is, there was still more than what meets the eye.*

His partner, Steve Vaughn, was as different as day and night from Fleming. The two had met by virtue of Vaughn's standing as a professional guide and leading expeditions into those areas that held little if any civilization. Wild areas with wild men and unsettled geology that could still swallow a man or a convoy in bottomless pits of quicksand. His close-cropped brown hair had the hint of gray starting to show through. Looking like a combination of a Russian weightlifter or circus strongman, his heavy chest was covered in a battered field jacket. Earth tone cotton-canvas cargo pants bloused over thick soled combat boots, completed his ensemble. He looked like a barroom brawler type, the kind with the philosophy of "Fight dirty, fight lazy. Why trade blows when you can stomp, kick or break?"

Michael decided Vaughn was the kind of man you wanted on your side and not the kind to have as an opponent. Vaughn said, "My services have been utilized for tracking people, finding lost hikers, pilots, downed experimental aircraft, etc., including long term remote surveillance of enemy camps, leading snipers and infiltration teams to remote enemy strongholds. Once in place, I then have provided security and overwatch. I have been in combat multiple times with enemy agents, bandits, land pirates, etc.

"You name it, the possibilities are endless, and if I haven't done it, I probably thought about doing it." Vaughn's weapons were Lancer remakes of the Ruger Super Redhawk in .454 Casull, Ruger Mark II pistol with an integral suppressed barrel and a Marlin lever action guide gun in .45-70. There was what appeared to be an ancient Cold Steel SRK survival knife and a Leatherman multi-tool. Michael decided the man could probably handle himself competently in either a shootout, knife or fist fight. He was one of two "medics" on Fleming's team.

Fleming hollered, "Sparks, come over here and introduce yourself!"

Chapter Fifty-Three

A man jogged over to where Michael and Bishop were. "Hi, I'm Sparks—real name is Patrick Haryett. I'm the IT for this group and our communications. I hold an advanced Ham radio license; that allows me to make all modifications and adjustments on our communications gear. I can fix most computer issues with my eyes closed and I have credentials as an electronics technician and dual trade welder/fabricator."

Fleming barked, "He's our jack-of-all-trades and master of none. He can fix a carbureted engine blindfolded and just about any mechanical issue on a vehicle with a piece of bailing wire and bubble gum, plus he is a machinist. He's good enough to do pretty much any home construction or repairs that are electrical, plumbing, framing, roofing or plasterboard."

Michael looked confused. "Plasterboard? What is that?"

Fleming smiled. "Sorry, we Brits call it plasterboard. You call it drywall."

"Two great countries separated by a common language," Michael said, smiling.

Fleming grinned and nodded. "Yeah, something like that."

"I'm not too bad in hand-to-hand either," Haryett smiled. "I double as a scout and did search and rescue for several years. Pretty much let me grab my backpack, drop me in the brush, and I'll see you in a week."

Michael heard a throaty exhaust approaching from behind and turned and jumped to one side as a blue and white Harley Davidson Heritage Soft Tail slid to a stop, showering him with dirt and gravel. Dressed in jeans and black riding leathers sat a bear of a man. Dark eyes stuck in a wind-weathered face, peering at him from behind a full bushy beard and mustache.

"What is, Brother?" a booming voice to match the man's size rumbled. "Sorry 'bout the dirt and gravel but I'm late and in a hurry. Neal James is the name." The bear unstraddled the Harley and squeezed Michael's hand in a brutal but unintentional death grip handshake.

Fleming smirked and said, "Sorry Mr. President, but we're lucky he's even here and sober. If he shows up at ten o'clock, he takes a break at eleven. Goes to lunch at noon, comes back at two. Takes breaks at three and four and then wants to get off at five o'clock."

The bear grinned. "Oh, and I don't work weekends or holidays and I need a company car and credit card. But I'm really, really cute. That's what matters. I should get this gig based on one thing—good looks 'cause I have very little talent. Oh, did I mention I can play the guitar and sing? Soooooo, when do I start?"

In a gesture Michael didn't expect from Fleming, Ryan Fleming grabbed the big bear of a man in a head lock and with a laugh said, "Sit down till we have introduced the whole team." *There is more to Mr. Fleming than meets the eye,* Michael thought.

Turning, Fleming said, "This is David Lynn, he's our magician."

Lynn stepped forward and extended his hand. He was probably the oldest man on the team with long gray hair and a gray beard. His eyes sparked as he said with a grin, "I make things. I cast replicas of items, people, whatever you need. Do you need a fake bomb made of foam rubber that weighs less than a pound and scrunches up under an armpit? Wonder how long air traffic would be held up with that. Or FX trauma to look like Ebola which would make most of your enemy leave the area... All safe of course, just things to fool the enemy.

"If any of the Rourke clan needs a body double to show at another location as an alibi in certain operations, not a problem. My casting studio... well, let's just say it is a place where we can meet and dream up what you might want and then take it with you to do battle in the real world. Plus," he added pulling off his backpack, "this carries everything I'd need to accomplish the same thing in the field."

Pointing across the clearing, Fleming waved and another man stood up. "This is Earl Burger, a military brat who spent sixteen years in the Air Force as a medic, most of it working in a Level One Trauma ER and teaching EMT classes, Advance Trauma Life Support classes, first aid and suturing. He was an EMT-I and served overseas."

Burger saluted Michael. "Sir, I also have worked with computers for a long time, used to do programming but my wife put a stop to that. She did not like the way I talked when I was programming. Think of a cross between a robot and an android. I even told her once that something was not logical. I only did that once and she told me to stop programming. She was also a medic in the military.

"In addition to the medical side, radios and computers, I give the rest of the team lessons in rock climbing and Scuba diving. I'm working on ground school, and I dabble in herbal medicine and work with wood and metal. I guess you could say I'm pretty heavy into survival or whatever else this team becomes involved with. Especially survival, my heavy training started when I was in high school.

"But even when I was younger I was the only one in my family that would still have Halloween candy at Easter and Easter candy on Halloween. I have six brothers and sisters so you could see how hard that would be. I was good at hiding my stash. I can and have adapted to live in different areas and cultures.

"Combat wise, I won the Schützenschnur when shooting with the Bundeswehr while stationed in New Germany. That's a marksmanship medal on a lanyard which is awarded by the Federal Republic of New Germany and it comes in three classes: gold, silver and bronze."

"Which one did you get?" Michael asked.

With a wry smile, Burger just said, "Well... I don't like to brag... The competition consisted of several shooting exercises with the G113, that's the latest version of the G3 battle rifle you might be familiar with. It uses the 7.92mmX40mm caseless round 155gr projectile, fifty round mags, built-in optics, add on 25mm grenade launcher with changeable 5-round revolving mag. It has a Bullpup stock with a 50cm barrel over all length 75cm, rate of fire 600 full auto or 2600 on three round burst, electric trigger and ignition. The front hand grip is designed to be able to attach the grenade launcher. Same trigger could be used with electrical connection and selector switch. We also used the heavy machine gun in competition.

"My sniper rifle is of my own design, uses 50 BMG like round caseless, with a sabot 35 caliber center of tungsten covered depleted uranium at 375gr. rail gun projectile accelerator on the barrel to bring the projectile up to 15,000 fps and has computer assisted optics. I like the Lancer versions of the old Gerber Mk I and Mk II, the old G3 and a long slide .45. I also like their version of the Desert Eagle using .45 Winchester Magnum rounds.

"Secondary handgun is the Lancer Model .357 RB, a remake of the stainless Ruger Blackhawk in .357. I have a few hot rounds I worked up for this that I would not let anyone else shoot in their .357. I would be afraid their gun would come apart. But don't get me wrong, I think that the only weapon you have is your brain—all else are just tools."

Fleming said, "Earl's a good guy but he's got a streak of vindictiveness. Tends to yell a lot but don't mind that. The time to worry is when he's calm and smiles at you."

Chapter Fifty-Four

Sullivan and his staff were working the details on finding John Rourke while the President was getting to know Unit 917—his "Posse." It was decided that the mission named Operation Hay Stack, would be divided into several elements. Four heavy submarines capable of underwater launches had been dispatched to the southeast coast of Alaska. They would be on station within eighteen hours and would cover roughly from what had been the border between Alaska and Canada's British Columbia, to the Cook Inlet near what had been Anchorage, Alaska.

Two heavy cruisers and four more heavy subs were steaming toward and along the southern edge of the Ice Cap that now covered all the way from the North Pole to past what had been the Aleutian Islands. Additionally a surface force and air support was being deployed to cover the areas around Hawaii and Mid-Wake. Coast defenses along the west coast of the Continental U.S. had already been placed on high alert and available satellites were being repositioned to allow for "real time" observation of the northern hemisphere.

The Egg, piloted by General Rodney Thorne, would be the lead element in the aerial campaign. It was The Egg's cloaking capability on which much of the success or failure of the mission rested. Four of the VTOL cargo planes would fly below The Egg, all shielded from sight and detection by The Egg's counter-illuminating camouflage technology. Within those cargo planes was the ground force equipment and personnel that would attempt to penetrate the defenses of the underground pyramid.

Scattered among the personnel would be the eight human pilots and four 442nd clones that had been trained, or as in the case of the 442nd personnel, retrained to operate the Alien UFOs. One, Akiro Kuriname, rode with Thorne in The Egg. The other eleven, once disembarked from the cargo craft, would be distributed so that no two were assigned to the same unit or vehicle. This allowed for the greatest possible survival rate among the pilots.

Once the aerial component reached its mark, the four VTOL cargo planes were to split up and head to the area around each of the two tunnel mouths and disembark all vehicles and personnel, while The Egg attempted to monitor the skies for intrusion and try to manipulate the counter-illuminating camouflage technology to continue to cover the planes.

On paper it looked tight, but Sullivan knew that "if something could go wrong, it would go wrong and always at the worst possible time." And he knew, to quote that dynamic World War II leader, General George Patton, "No plan survives first contact with the enemy and the enemy always gets a vote." He did not consider this a pessimistic viewpoint but rather a realistic one. He had his own saying, "If you can't see the fault in your plan, count on the fact your enemy will."

What was the weakness in this plan? The biggest was that he had zero intelligence on what to expect inside either the tunnels or the pyramid and no perceivable way to get any. Then an idea hit him. Picking up his phone he dialed a number.

"Hello."

"This is General Sullivan, Sir. Could I impose on you to come to my office for a moment?"

"Certainly."

Chapter Fifty-Five

"So there you are, that's my idea," Sullivan said. "Could you make it happen?"

The Keeper sat, frowning. He stood and paced back and forth several times, finally saying, "Honestly, General... I don't know. I have tried repeatedly over the past weeks to make contact with John Rourke. Except for some vague tingling sensations and ambiguous images... I have failed. I can attempt it but truthfully, I don't have much hope."

Sullivan snorted, "Damnit!" He slammed his fist down hard on the desk. "We are blind as church mice."

The Keeper smiled. "Wait a moment... General. If my memory is accurate, the members of the 442nd were clones originally sent by the Aliens, correct?"

Sullivan nodded. "Yeah, the first one we captured was one of the Captain Dodd clones. Unfortunately, he died from mysterious causes under interrogation. John Rourke hypothesized there was some kind of connection between his death and the strange tattoo he wore. When the President's convoy was attacked later on, Rourke interrupted the clone who was trying to kill Michael Rourke. John Rourke used a combat knife and excised the tattoo after the clone had been knocked unconscious. He recovered and that is now the man you know as Akiro Kuriname."

The Keeper nodded. "And the rest of the 442nd personnel underwent a similar removal of their tattoos after the battle in the tunnel complex. Correct?"

Sullivan nodded. "Correct."

"However," The Keeper said again with a smile, "not all of those men were rehabilitated, correct?"

Again Sullivan nodded. "Correct, several died and one..." he stopped in mid thought. "And one was not put through the excising procedure. He was kept in total isolation and... his tattoo is intact!"

The Keeper smiled. "Yes it is General. I think it is time I meet the diabolical Captain Timothy Dodd."

Chapter Fifty-Six

The Ambrose Federal Detention Center, part of the maximum security federal prison system, the AFDC, named for former state Senator Malcolm Ambrose, was under the operational control of the Federal Bureau of Prisons, a division of the United States Department of Justice. It had added a new wing. It was five stories high and ultra secure; what had come to be called Ultra Max. There was only one prisoner and he was housed on the top floor. His cell was exactly in the middle of that floor with a complex series of cages and gates which could be controlled, opened or closed, electronically or manually.

The fourth floor held a medical ward, exclusively for that one prisoner and a clinic for the personnel responsible for the care and welfare of that one prisoner. There were no windows on this floor and the same complex series of cages and gates existed to move from the fourth floor to the third. Both floors had been constructed with a delivery system that could flood the area with an oneirogenic general anesthetic in the event of a disturbance.

Oneirogenic general anesthetic is the formal name for sleeping gas, an incapacitating agent used to place a subject in a state of unconsciousness so that they are not aware of what is happening around them. Often it is used to keep a person from harming themselves or others. Most sleeping gases have undesirable side effects, and are only effective at doses that approach toxicity. The gas used in this situation was odorless, colorless and tasteless so as not to alert its victims.

The third floor was a cafeteria and recreation center complete with a small gym, all dedicated to the personnel responsible for the care and welfare of that one prisoner. The second floor was a dormitory for the four shifts of personnel responsible for the care and welfare of that one prisoner. The last and final floor was the ground or first floor. It was a series of cages and gates which could be controlled electronically or manually from a control room on the north side of that floor.

There were three exit doors. One led to the exercise yard which was triple fenced. The first and second fences were electrified and covered at the top with razor wire. The third was separated from the second by fifteen feet of concrete pavement with four watch towers, each containing a guard with an automatic rifle.

The second door was the normal portal for entrance and exit, the third was an emergency door only opened in extreme situations. The door frame contained blocks of high explosives which could be detonated from either the control rooms electronically or manually by failing to put the proper code in to activate that door.

Ultra Max.

Captain Timothy Dodd sat on his bunk listening to classical music, especially chosen for its calming nature. Over the months since his incarceration, his day never changed. The routine of his meals rotated once every ten days. At first the rotation had seemed random but with sufficient study, he had figured out the schedule. After all it was simply a mathematical problem. And Captain Timothy Dodd, at least this facsimile of the long dead Timothy Dodd, was every bit as intelligent and creative as his parent. He also was every bit as dangerous and patient.

He had known on day one that he had a distinct advantage over his guards. They had a job, they had families and friends and they had another world to go to when they left at the end of their shift. He did not.

He, on the other hand, had two things they did not: focus and time. Combining those with an intellect that had won his parent an astronaut rating and the equivalent rank of a full Colonel, and the patience of a rock... well, it was not a question of would he win. It was a question of when and how big would he win.

His cell was monitored by cameras 24/7. So was the shower and latrine. The fact that no guard was allowed to speak to him, nor was he allowed to have tools, tobacco, pencil, paper or silverware or plates except for Styrofoam and only one plastic Spork—a combination spoon, fork and knife made of plastic—had made his mission difficult but not impossible.

Today, he noticed something that did not fit with the mind numbing tranquility of his cell. There had been an ever so slight shift in the stillness of the air. Ever... so... slight...

Chapter Fifty-Seven

The Little Sac River still ran along the northeast side of the Caverns before it ultimately emptied into the Sac River. In the old days, the basin was chiefly rural. Land use was primarily pasture and grazing, with the rest divided between forest, row crop, and urban land development. Animal agriculture was the major enterprise in the basin with beef cattle and dairy production being predominant.

Today the land lay fallow; no farming or crops had been on it for a long time. Normally this was done on purpose to allow the soil to regain its fertility. In this case, it had been done because there was no one left to plow the land.

Paul and the Dog Soldiers had gone over the edge of the gorge that was home to the Little Sac and worked their way back up river. Twice they had come to areas that were blocked by landslides of rocks and boulders. Their process was slow, the team walking and picking its way along the bottom of the riverbed could only move so far then have to stop to allow the surface teams to reposition the twelve counter-illuminated camouflage generators.

Unless the search area parameters changed significantly, that only took a few minutes. Several times, however, it took well over an hour to make the adjustments to the cloaking field. The first day was fast ending; the search would have to take second place to setting up camp. Wes Sanderson made the decision to bring the search team up to the top of the gullies.

He established a defensive parameter within which the eight Armored All-Terrain Vehicles were parked. Communication equipment was set up and each team was responsible for setting up tents, sleeping bags and getting each member fed. Paul sat with Kuriname going over the aerial photos of the area.

"Akiro," Paul said. "We have to be right on top of the Cavern. That's the only thing that makes sense."

"Could there have been more movement and collapse than you thought?"

Paul shook his head. "Sure, anything is possible but I just don't think so. There are still too many hard landmarks visible. Look, right here on the aerial photo, that is part of the old road which brought people to the cavern; problem is it stops right here. I'm guessing we're less than a mile from the mouth of the cave."

"Well, if we are that close, we will find it tomorrow, my friend."

"We will have to find it sooner than later, that is for sure. I can't move on to Phase Two until we do."

Chapter Fifty-Eight

Akiro had been correct in his guess. The search team had only gone about fifty yards up the gorge when one of the men called a halt. Pulling binoculars from his pack, he scanned the left side of the gully near the top. "Mr. Rubenstein," he called. "Can you come here a second?" Paul jogged over and the man handed him the binoculars. "Left side, maybe forty feet from the very top. Do you see that black line running horizontally?"

Paul strained his eyes. "Wait a minute," he said and adjusted his position in the gully several feet to the left. "Yes, now I see it. You have good eyes Trooper. I really thought the opening would be in the gorge itself." Paul keyed his microphone directing the surface team to that location.

Sanderson called back ten minutes later. "Mr. Rubenstein, you need to get up here."

"Throw a line, will ya?"

Sanderson secured the line to a tree and hollered, "Look out below."

The coil of rope unrolled perfectly. *How did he do that?* Paul wondered. *Every time I have tried that, the rope gets all knotted up around itself.* Ten minutes later Paul pulled himself over the top edge of the gully and grabbed Sanderson's extended hand. With a jerk and a heave, Paul was topside and untying the rope. "Wes," Paul said. "You have to teach me the secret to throwing a roll of rope like that sometime."

Sanderson laughed and said simply, "Lots and lots of practice combined with the natural athletic ability of a professional Marine."

Paul smiled and followed Sanderson to the cliff face. There had been a collapse and ground slippage long ago, but from under the lip of the cliff there was a stretch of blacktop still visible for a few inches. Paul turned left and walked to the top of a small rise. Pushing through the tall grass he found what he was looking for. A concrete pad.

"This was the base of the old gift shop and office. Let me get my bearings. Across that field is where there used to be a couple of outbuildings which were used for equipment storage and maintenance." Paul closed his eyes and was remembering when he heard a shout.

"Over here, down on the next level," one of the Dog Soldiers shouted. Paul clambered down slipping twice but not falling. "Take a look at this." There were the remnants of a rusted chunk of metal and a large gear wheel, probably two feet in diameter.

"I know what that is," Paul said. "That is part of the old steam engine used to power the cave lights in the early days. Paul shut his eyes trying to drag the memory closer to him. He could see their guide, Ken. Was that his name? Ken... no." In his mind's eye he could see the man's name tag. "No, not Ken... Kirk," Paul mumbled to himself. "Nice guy."

He opened his eyes and turned to the right. "Wes, I need two teams. One right here with shovels and machetes. I want to clear the vegetation away from that hill face. Another on the other side where I came up. Let's get some jacks, flashlights and rope. We have found the Fantastic Caverns, now let see if we can get into it."

Sanderson nodded and started issuing orders but the first order he issued was to move the AATVs to this location and set up the counter-illuminated camouflage generators. Paul sat down with a smile on his face. If he closed his eyes just right, he could almost see the place the way it was so long ago. And he could almost see his parents' faces. Absently, he wiped away a single tear as he stood up and pulled a shovel out of the back of the nearest AATV.

Chapter Fifty-Nine

"Okay, gentlemen," said the guard as he monitored Captain Dodd's cell. "He is out."

"How do you know he is not faking?" Blackman asked.

The guard pointed at a small screen to the left of the television screen they had been watching. "You see those readings? Those show the rate of his breathing and heartbeat, there are a number of laser devices focused on his cell. They detect and measure the elements of the parasympathetic nervous system and sympathetic nervous system. The first one controls homeostasis and the body at rest and is responsible for the body's 'rest and digest' function. The second controls the body's responses to a perceived threat and is responsible for the 'fight or flight' response. Both are part of the autonomic nervous system which is responsible for the involuntary functions of the human body. In other words, he can't fake them."

The Keeper said to Blackman, "Please monitor them exactly, if there is the slightest change, no matter how minute, I must stop what I am doing or we will be discovered."

"I understand," Blackman said. "Go ahead."

The Keeper moved to the corner of the control room and sat on the floor facing away from both the guard and Blackman. His breathing became deeper and more rhythmic, his eyes closed and he sent his thoughts out into the universe, *John, where are you? Are you there?* He tried this over and over until it became a mantra.

He turned to Blackman, "Still no contact, going to the second subject." Blackman nodded. The Keeper went back into his deep breathing and closed his eyes as he reached out with his mind. Something in the universe stirred; The Keeper sent one word out mentally, *Remember.*

Chapter Sixty

By the time he broke contact with Dodd, The Keeper's face was covered in a sheen of sweat. Blackman handed him a paper towel and The Keeper wiped his face and hands. "Well?" Blackman said.

"Very interesting," The Keeper said. "Not at all what I expected, knowing this subject's history."

"What did you see... or feel... or whatever it is you do?"

The Keeper shook his head. "I think I should wait until we are with the General if you don't mind, Doctor."

*****

"So," said Sullivan. "Our Captain Dodd was part of the... I don't know what to even call it... the Alien Air Wing?"

"I did not get an impression of what it is called, General," The Keeper said. "But, yes. I would say that is correct and, from what I saw, the remainder of the craft are housed in the pyramid. The vehicles launch and recover via these tunnels and counting the ones destroyed during the attack on the Capital while Michael's inauguration was going on, I think between ten and fifteen remain."

"Didn't get an exact number?"

The Keeper shook his head. "Couldn't. Rather than probing for specifics, it was like I was passively watching memories as they replayed for Captain Dodd. Very much like watching him dream."

Sullivan nodded. "Just how accurate do you think those impressions are?"

"I think they accurately show what Dodd saw. Let me explain. What I saw was through Dodd's eyes, but sometimes filtered by his emotions, his wants and his desires. I saw The Creator, or at least Dodd's picture of him, not... not exactly what I pictured. Much more... benign, I suppose would be a good word. What I registered most were the feelings that Dodd had when The Creator was around. The Creator was having a tremendous impact on Dodd. His anxiety dropped, his agitation lessened, the normal tension in his body seemed to melt away."

"And that is very similar to some of the readings we had with the 442nd people," Blackman said. "Not the... malevolent impression of a conqueror I expected."

"Nor I," agreed The Keeper. "More like a scholar or a scientist."

"What else?" Sullivan asked.

"Nothing about John Rourke," The Keeper said. "But that does not surprise me. Captain Dodd has been in captivity since before Rourke disappeared."

"What else?"

The Keeper shook his head. "It is not so much what I saw and heard and felt but what I did not. No militant structure, no rushing around or 'defensive posturing' and no... I guess concern would be a good word. Everything I saw had a very peaceful orientation."

"You reported there might be captives from what you saw with the 442nd people."

The Keeper nodded. "There are humans there but I am not sure we should label them captives. They appear to move around freely and without encumbrance."

Sullivan stood and walked to his window and gazed out for some time; processing. Finally he said, "So, from your vision of Dodd and the 442nd folks... everything seems, I don't know. Copasetic?" The Keeper and Blackman nodded. "Any idea how and if you might be able to make contact directly with The Creator, or at least tap into its awareness?"

"'IT' is a good description," said The Keeper. "I have no impression of gender. I have no impression this species even has gender. I don't think trying to surreptitiously 'tap in' would be smart. It might be construed as an attack."

"Or a sign of disrespect," Blackman added.

The Keeper shook his head. "No, not disrespect. That is an emotional response. Captain Dodd's interactions with the creature do not paint an emotional picture. Rather, almost a raw intellect above the level of an emotion. Very black or white, right or wrong, very..." He searched for the word.

"Very binary?" Sullivan asked.

"Exactly! Very binary."

"Like in mathematics or digital electronics," Sullivan said, smiling. "A system that represents numeric values using only two symbols, typically zero and one. Just like a computer."

Chapter Sixty-One

Gaining entrance to the cave was both easier and more complicated than Paul had imagined. Easier because the vegetation and dirt near the entrance by the old steam generator was a lot easier to remove than he thought it would be. It took less than two hours before there was a hole big enough for a man to crawl through in the dirt barrier.

"Holy Crap," the volunteer named Jackson hollered. "There is a door here, a metal door!" As the rest of the team continued to assault the dirt barrier, they could hear the 'bong, bong' of a fist striking the metal door. Then there was a loud 'skreach' that sounded like the cry of a banshee or a lost soul falling into the underworld. Everyone stopped what they were doing.

A moment later, Johnson crawled back out of what remained of the dirt barrier. "Mr. Rubenstein," he said and handed Paul his flashlight. "I think you should be the first one in."

Paul took the light, thanked the man and said, "Come on then, you'll be the second." Shouting over his shoulder, Paul said, "Get the rest of this dirt moved and be ready to go in! We will be right back!" Then both men slipped from view into the bowels of the earth.

Shovels and picks attacked the barrier which was now hardly more than a dirt pile. By the time fifteen minutes had passed, even the dirt pile was gone. The metal door made another loud "skreach" and the two men came out of the dark with big smiles on their faces.

"It is even better than I thought!" Paul said. "Wes, this is your part but I would suggest we get everybody that is going in roped together just for safety's sake. How's it coming on the other side?"

Sanderson shook his head. "That side is going to take longer. More rock to move and less dirt. We are using some of the AATVs to move the bigger pieces." He turned to Haskins. "Sergeant, hot foot it over there and tell Kuriname I want a security detail over there. Send the rest over here and link up a good security line that will cover both entrances. I want listening observation posts on top of this hill and on the far side of the gully. When we have the area secured… tell him we are going spelunking."

"Roger that Chief," Haskins said and took off at a dead run.

Sanderson pointed to another NCO. "Let's break out the lights and the generators, I want to have some power going into this hole in the ground before sunset. Tonight, we will have hot meals; I want a cook fire set up at the entrance of the cave. I think we should have a little celebration tonight."

Paul had walked away from the group, carrying an encrypted keypad. He typed in a message to his brother-in-law, Michael Rourke. "Phase one complete" and hit send. A moment later a response pinged. "Congratulations. When will you start Phase Two?"

Paul typed, "Day after tomorrow" and sent the message. For the first time in many days he had hope for the future again.

Chapter Sixty-Two

The last few members of the Posse were gathered around Michael and Bishop. "This is Michael Spivey," Fleming said, as another man walked up. "He is one of our more reasonable team members. You could say he's one of the more stable ones. Been married to the same lady forever, they have three children now all adults and two grandchildren. I have no idea how his wife and family put up with him."

"Thanks Boss," Spivey said. "Before my reputation is slandered anymore let me tell you the truth. I'm a vet, Navy, and saw combat as an Armed Civilian Combatant accompanying US Armed Forces on a couple of operations. I worked for a while in something you might have heard of called the resurrected 'Skunk Works' special weapons units. If you don't know what it is I can't tell you—it's classified.

"I was a Boy Scout; actually I'm a Life Scout and a Sea Explorer, Quartermaster. I'm an archer, and a bower, building both bows and arrows. I have been studying Martial Arts since I was twelve and currently hold Advanced Black Belt ranks in Tang Soo Do Moo Duk Kwan, Fifth Degree Black Belt; Toyama Ryu Batto Jutsu, Fourth Degree Black Belt; and Daito Ryu Aikijujutsu, Fourth Degree Black Belt, with lower ranking in other Martial Arts including Arnis/Escrima, Muay Thai, Savate, Kung Fu, and Wu Tai Chi."

Fleming said, "At his age and experience he has probably forgotten more about hand to hand than most people know exists. Attack him and any of the following or a combination of things will have occurred in less than five seconds: An attacker will not be able to get air in or out of their lungs, they will not be able to hear, their clavicles will be broken. Shoulders will be dislocated, elbows will be bent the wrong way and their spine will no longer be attached to the skull. Their hips, knees or ankles will no longer work; the spine will be severely injured. Against a knife when one is empty handed, one must expect to get cut unless the attacker is a total incompetent."

"So you know how to use a knife?" Michael asked.

"Knife or blade work is not what one sees pictured in the movies. In general what is forgotten is there is a hand attached to that knife, and that hand/wrist/arm is your target, NOT the body, which is the secondary target. Put a sword or stick, or sticks, in my hand and unless one is more proficient than me, which is possible but not probable, the attacker would be better off to just leave.

"Working with what's his name over there," Spivey said, pointing at Harker, "we keep the team functioning mechanically. I'm a Journeyman Machinist, welder and Ham Radio operator. I can tell you I'm a gunsmith and pistolsmith; I research, design and build firearms. I'm also a blacksmith, cabinetmaker and a swordsman.

"I am both a long distance and a combat rifleman, and I enjoy hunting and fishing. I am a Mountain Man/Fur Trade reenactor, gardener and teach a small group of students Martial Arts. Anything else, I'll keep to myself until I've seen your security clearance myself. Now, just who the hell are you?"

"Me, oh… I'm really not anyone special. My name's Michael Rourke, proud to meet you guys."

"You're Michael Rourke?" the last man exclaimed, whipping off his floppy Boonie hat and standing up quickly from sitting on a bulging rucksack. "THE Michael Rourke? Wow!"

Fleming introduced the last member of the team, of average height and build, freckled with a shaved head and a short red and graying beard. Rourke observed that he wore a .45 caliber Sig Sauer P220 and a Cold Steel Kukri on his hips, plus a load bearing vest stuffed with spare pistol mags and medical supplies, over a dark t-shirt and khaki cargo pants. "This is Jim, full name— James Elton Judy the Third."

Jim rolled his eyes and chuckled at the sound of his full name. "Also known as 'Doc' by the troops. His formal training provided him by the Navy, he saw duty with Fleet Hospitals, 1st Battalion 5th Marines, 1st Light Armored Reconnaissance, to mention a few, and he's another EMT on the team."

Jim continued, "I was a Navy Hospital Corpsman, Mr. Rourke, and I earned the moniker 'Doc,' once my Marines accepted me as one of their own. While with the Infantry, I went out of my way to provide medical coverage on every rifle, pistol, and shotgun training course that I could. They taught me as well, and after a while I was considered by my Master Gunnery Sergeant and the training team as an 'unofficial but qualified' range instructor.

"If it's issued to the troops, I can shoot it and probably teach you to shoot it. I've also received urban and close quarters combat, survival, cold weather and mountain warfare training and have put all of those skills to work." With the toe of his heavy hiking boot, he nudged the large weathered rucksack at his feet. "I've got everything I need to survive, and help others stay alive, in ol' Bessie here.

"After leaving the Navy, I was a bit of a leaf in the wind. I had a bit of a hippie phase and became a meditation and yoga instructor, and began teaching and traveling. I also worked as a long haul truck driver, transporting needed materials across what was left of the U.S. If it's big, I can drive it. I've seen more of the country than probably anyone I know, and I have friends and contacts all over. Somehow along the way, I picked up Bachelor of Arts degrees in English and Philosophy, and have worked formally as a school teacher.

"I'm yet another resident martial arts enthusiast, beginning in my teens and including Bujinkan 2nd Dan and various others including Pencak Silat, Eskrima, Muay Thai, Judo, Brazilian Jiu Jitsu, and military combatives of course. If it works, I'll use it, I'm not picky. I'm not quite as experienced or as… ahem… enthusiastic as Mr. Spivey over there, but I can hang." He patted the weapons on his hips. "Nobody messes with my team or my patients."

Jim stepped forward and shook Michael's hand. "I did not have my father there when I was a child and stories of John Rourke and you filled me when I was most impressionable. I'm very honored to meet you, Sir. You guys inspired me to be a good father. My wife and I have two girls that we take hiking and camping all the time. My Lady comes from a long line of Girl Scouts and she raises the kids in the Scout tradition, giving them the skills to be self-reliant wherever they may be."

Suddenly, there were sounds of turmoil coming from the brush surrounding the camp. There was a howling, joined by another further off and a reverberation like lions charging the camp. Michael turned as Fleming stepped forward. "Hold it, Sir. It's okay, just the last two members of my team showing up."

Two small dogs bounded into the clear. "Mr. President, meet Fugi and Goeman. Best trackers you ever saw and smarter than the rest of the team combined. Goeman trained Fugi the Wonder Pup, she's female. He has trained a whole host of dogs back at headquarters in the art of self-reliance, jumping, and penetrating human camps to locate stores, hostages or victims. The breed, Shetland Sheepdog, is historically used for herding and watchdog functions, but they do a lot more for us.

"They have their own assault harnesses, can carry not only their gear but can help carry that of others, just not too much; they only weigh about twenty pounds apiece! They are really good guard dogs, and can track bears and coyotes from a long way away. They can sense good people from bad, and make really great advance scouts. They can live off the land, but don't leave any unguarded dinner plates or take-out Chinese food," Fleming said, laughing.

"Their trainers, Joe and Nikki, volunteered to let me put them on the team when it's necessary. To be honest, I don't think about the team going into the field anymore without these two. I think it was Joe that said once, 'These guys will cross the Rainbow Bridge, and wait for the rest of you to catch up.'"

Chapter Sixty-Three

Horst Burkholter and Helmut Freed watched the video screen. The small, nearly silent aerial drone's high resolution camera gave an excellent picture. Burkholter pointed to the two fifteen-man teams that approached the training area. "This is perfect Helmut, we will kill the President while he is watching the training exercise and make it look like a terrible training accident," Burkholter said with a smile.

"Finally," Freed said, "the death of your brother Johann and the maiming of my brother Franz by the bastard John Rourke will be avenged."

Burkholter shook his head, "They will not be avenged until ALL of the Rourkes are dead but this will be the start. The attack on Sarah Rourke-Mann and John Rourke's wife Emma failed, we will not fail. Michael Rourke dies today and then we will hunt the rest of the family down with the help of Peter Vale and his operatives."

Freed smiled. "And these soldiers... What of them?"

Burkholter snorted. "Collateral damage, nothing more. Watch, it begins..."

*****

Michael Rourke and Sergeant Major Bishop turned and started back to the tent that served as the Command Post for the exercise area. Bishop caught a flash of reflected light out of the corner of his eye; he spun and launched himself at the President, knocking him to the ground.

"What the..." Michael shouted then heard the report of a rifle shot and the whine of a .308 round cut the air above the two of them.

Ryan Fleming realized immediately what was happening, he saw men moving in the tree line where none of his people were supposed to be. Quickly assessing the situation, he pointed at the armored personnel carrier and shouted to Bishop, "Get the President to the APC!" Then he blew three quick blasts on the whistle that dangled on a cord around his neck.

Across the compound, magazines with blank ammunition were ejected to fall on the ground. Each of the POTUS POSSE had two magazines of live rifle ammo and three of live pistol ammo in special carriers on their load bearing harnesses. In less time than it takes to describe it, the Posse transformed from a training mission to a real world fire fight.

Fleming's six foot nine frame gave him an advantage; his hand signals were easily spotted across the open ground. He was also at a disadvantage and soon found himself becoming a bullet magnet. He ripped the useless bandoliers of 20-round training magazines off his chest and slammed home a mag of live rounds into the Lancer Model M1A1 .308 rifle. *Have to make this count, I only have forty rounds*, he thought as he ran to a gully for cover. Rolling into the gully, he quickly rammed live ammo into the .45 pistol and opened fire with well-aimed shots.

Steve Vaughn landed next to Fleming, "What the hell, Boss?" Vaughn levered the blanks out of his Marlin guide gun and thumbed live .45-70 rounds into it. The big gun belched fire and one of the attackers was picked up and thrown several feet backwards; when he hit the ground he didn't move.

"Boss," a voice called from the left, it was Patrick Haryett, one of the communications specialists. Fleming acknowledged with a hand signal as Haryett signaled back that he, Neal James, and David Lynn were going to circle around to the left side. Fleming acknowledged and turned to Vaughn. "We're sitting ducks. We have to get organized and right now."

Vaughn sent a 300 grain slug out the end of his barrel at a speed of 2400 feet per second. When it slammed into the chest of an attacker a little over one hundred yards away, it was still doing about 2,000 feet per second. "I'm headed over to the ditch over there," Vaughn said, pointing to the right. "I'll grab a couple of guys and try to circle around to that side."

Fleming nodded. "Take Burger if you can find him, but you'll need to have a medic with you."

Vaughn smiled. "What I'll need is that .50 caliber sniper rifle of his." Vaughn popped his head above the edge of the gully, did a quick look around and ducked back just as a slug tore into the ground. Wiping dust out of his eyes he said, "Yeah I spotted Burger, Spivey and Jim Judy over there."

Fleming nodded. "Tell Judy to stay there. He and I will keep the bloody bastards busy."

Vaughn nodded and said, "Cover me."

Fleming yelled, "Fire!" and lead filled the air as Vaughn raced across open ground. One round grazed his left shoulder and another went through a pant leg but missed meat. Breathing heavy, he dropped into the ditch. Fleming heard running steps behind him and Sergeant Major Bishop and Michael Rourke leaped into the gully with him. Fleming yelled, "Bloody hell... I told you to get him to the APC! Sergeant Major I didn't take you for an arse."

"I heard you and I had him in the APC," Bishop said, smiling. "And that's where we found these M-16s, a box of live ammo for each, and these little toys. Want one?" Bishop pitched Fleming a hand grenade. "I would have kept the President there Mr. Fleming but he outranks me."

"Will you two stop talking about me and talk to me," Michael said. "Last time I looked I was the Boss not some piece of luggage to be protected. Ryan, give me a SITREP."

Fleming realized he wasn't going to win this argument and nodded. "Looks like we've been attacked by twenty to thirty men; eight of those were downed by our return fire. Haryett, James and David Lynn were going to circle around to the left. Vaughn is about to move to the right with Burger and Spivey. That leaves Jim Judy and the three of us in the center. All he has is his Sig .45 pistol; he is deadly up close but the bad guys are pretty much out of range, and Bob is your uncle."

"Bob is your what? What are you saying?" Bishop asked.

Fleming smiled and fired, dropping a bad guy before answering. "This is a well-used phrase. It is added to the end of sentences a bit like 'and that's it!'"

Rourke nodded. "Okay, Bishop and I were able to get a message out on the APC's communications net. Backup is only about fifteen minutes out."

"Blimey, that is good news." Fleming said. "The bleeding hell of it is I don't think we have fifteen minutes... here the bastards come!"

Vaughn, Burger and Spivey had only made about a hundred yards when the attackers began to move forward. Vaughn, behind a tree stump, squeezed off well aimed shots with his lever gun. Each hit was marked by flailing arms and legs and an eruption of red/pink gore as the heavy slug ripped through a torso and exploded head or throat. He quickly went through the seven rounds on the ammo cuff around the butt of his stock plus the five on his sling. The snap open ammo carriers on his belt only had ten rounds each for a total of twenty. Then it would be hand to hand... if they got the chance.

Burger's .50 caliber rifle had the reach on anything the bad guys had, and he had the penetration. One slug passed through the gut of one attacker, the chest of a second and still destroyed the head of a third. Burger watched unbelieving through his scope. *I'll be damned,* he thought. *No one is gonna believe that shot. I'm not sure I do.* But he knew sometimes in war strange things happen, and every now and then the good guys win one.

Spivey was out of ammo and locked in hand-to-hand combat with one of the attackers. Spivey had jumped the guy when he tried to change magazines, figuring to make quick work of him and take his weapon. Their initial contact had been fast and furious; the guy was good. Spivey thought, *Best laid plans of mice and men...* The guy attacked hard and fast. Spivey took a combination of front, side and roundhouse kicks and blocked them all but his foot caught on a root and he crashed to the ground, face down. Instantly his opponent was on him hammering the back of his head with fists. Spivey's mouth was full of dirt and debris, he couldn't see and he couldn't move. *I'm gonna die,* he thought.

Suddenly the attack stopped and the man fell off Spivey's back. Spivey pushed up, spitting dirt and leaves, trying to catch his breath. Wiping his eyes he found his attacker lying on his back behind him. His head looked like a deflated beach ball. Most of the skull and all of the brains had exited out the back when Burger's .50 slug hit. Spivey looked over to thank Burger but Burger was already sighted in on another attacker.

Haryett, James and David Lynn had silently made it around to the rear of the enemy force before opening fire. As the attackers rose up and started the charge down the hill, they opened up on them.

The attackers ran into withering fire from the front also. Finally, they were within range of Jim Judy's .45 and he calmly popped one and then another and then another. Bishop pulled the hand grenade pins then handed them to Rourke and Fleming. His arms were no longer capable of long range throws. When the grenades were gone, 5.56 tumblers cut down the rest of the attackers.

*****

By the time the reinforcements arrived, it was over. Haryett and Vaughn's team had checked the attackers making sure there was no longer a threat. They reported back to Fleming that several appeared to have taken their own lives rather than be captured and interrogated.

"That is a shame," Michael said. "We need Intel. We need to get ahead of these bastards. I'll bet you money that hit was planned by the same ones who killed Wolfgang Mann in New Germany."

Fleming smiled and put his hand on Michael's shoulder. "Look, this was a botch job. These fools should have taken us out. They were in place and had the element of surprise. Lucky for us they weren't that good, clumsy... work not of a high standard. We'll get another go at them. Anyone who says we won't win this... well, that's bullocks." There was a rustle from the brush and the dog Fuji came out with blood on his face and side. Fleming dropped down and checked the dog. The blood wasn't his. "Fugi, where is Goeman? Take us to Goeman."

Fugi barked and ran off; they found Goeman about twenty yards away. A stray bullet had creased Goeman's skull; the dog was unconscious but not seriously injured. Fugi had stayed with Goeman and protected him with his own body.

*****

"Mr. President," Sullivan said into the telephone receiver. "What do you think of your Posse?"

"Frankly, I'm impressed. Before the incident, I was a little confused about their necessity and function," Michael Rourke admitted. "But, after the attack, I see your point."

"It is really simple, Mr. President," Sullivan said. "Think of them as super Secret Service agents. They function when and if you are in the field. They will function whether or not you are still in office. They are people I have personally worked with and can attest to their skills and most importantly their loyalty."

"General, how can they be loyal to me? I just met them."

Sullivan laughed, "Not to you, Sir. To me. They will take their daily instructions from you but their mission comes directly from me."

"And exactly what is their mission?" Michael asked. "Hit men? Vigilantes? What?"

Sullivan grew quiet before answering slowly, "To keep you alive, Sir, no matter what."

Chapter Sixty-Four

The metal door that had been behind the dirt barrier was actually part of a wall which gave the entrance an almost bunker-like appearance. Paul remembered Kirk Hansen telling their tour group that during bad weather, especially tornados, people used the first room as a shelter.

The first room was large with a ceiling only seven feet in some places and a floor that angled up a steep slope and cresting with stalagmites. They moved on about fifty feet to an even larger area with a ceiling close to twenty-five feet in height and the floor was wider also. It was in these first two rooms that someone had tried to grow mushrooms in the early 1900s.

Paul said, "Keep your eyes open for bats. In the old days, there weren't any but there may be some in here now and watch those pools off to the side. Everyone keep to the hard surface area until we have had some time to explore a little more."

The rest of the cave floor was smooth with gentle slopes and pretty wide in some spots. Paul knew that while it felt like they were staying on a level surface, the cave actually was going downhill. Ahead were the remnants of an ancient wooden stage where presentations and even country western music was played. Off to the left side, and in one place on the right side, they could hear fast water moving through the lower level of the cave. Wiring hung in several places from the roof of the cave where lights had illuminated the pathways before The Night of the War.

Several of the old propane trams, converted jeeps that pulled cars with bench seats loaded with passengers for the cave tours, now stood empty in a row. Paul wondered whether or not they could be made to run again.

"What the hell is that?" someone asked.

Paul looked in the direction of the light. A round pipe came out of the ceiling and went into the floor. "That's an old water well from the twentieth century." They walked on for probably another quarter mile before turning back. Paul said, "Keep to the left on the way out and that will take us to the other entrance we found. We may have an easier time moving the debris from inside." That didn't work out, however, and the group had to back track a hundred yards or so and exit the way they had come in.

Kuriname was waiting on them when they came out. "Well, what did you think of it?"

Sanderson smiled. "Truly something to see. Why don't you get your people and take a tour, I'll send one of my folks with you as a guide. Seems safe enough but keep your people tied together and come out the way you went in. Sergeant Haskins," Sanderson called out.

"Yo."

"How about leading Captain Kuriname's group back for a quick tour?"

"Roger that Chief, happy to." Haskins turned to Akiro. "Your folks ready, Sir? Everyone got a flashlight?"

Akiro nodded. "Lead on Sergeant, we'll follow you."

"Let's go then," Haskins said. He took the lead but stopped and turned around. "Every third man keep your flashlight off. I want to have enough lights that have fresh batteries to find our way out. If the lights go out in there, it's darker than fifteen shades of hell."

Chapter Sixty-Five

Michael was sitting alone in his office with a pad and pen. He had been there for three hours making lists of names, changing it again and again until he finally leaned back and said, "Okay." He scanned the list. It held the names of the people he trusted most in the government and military. In total there were three lists of names. The first list were those he trusted. The second were those he felt were in the position or had the loyalty to sacrifice the lives they had and disappear. That meant extended families, careers... everything. It would be like entering the old Witness Protection Program the U.S. Marshalls had created back before The Night of the War. The third list was those that "could" or "might" be needed for the specific missions but not for full inclusion.

Once in, there would be no way out until it was time to reappear. Until that time they, all of them... everyone on that list would be declared rogues and would be hunted by those who would seize the government once the plan was instituted. Michael knew there was no way to avoid the loss of freedom and the shift of power that would come. His only hope was that if they were successful there would be a point in time when the government of the people, by the people and for the people, could be reinstituted in what remained of the United States of America.

There were questions that caused him consternation. One, could it all be done? Two, how long would it take? Could he find his father and could he find him in time. The final questions, and the most vexing... was he doing the right thing and was he doing it the right way?

"Only time will tell," Michael said to himself as he walked to the window. "You will only know the outcome after time has passed. Who knows what the future will bring? Sooner or later the truth, the reality will become known or be revealed. The future is unknown until it happens." Michael paused, a smile slowly crossing his lips. "What was that poem she wrote?" he said aloud as he walked to the bookshelf and found the volume he sought. Flipping quickly through the pages, he came to it. "Here it is." He read it to himself then turned back to his empty office and read it aloud:

"Life is an opportunity, benefit from it.

Life is beauty, admire it.

Life is a dream, realize it.

Life is a challenge, meet it.

Life is a duty, complete it.

Life is a game, play it.

Life is a promise, fulfill it.

Life is sorrow, overcome it.

Life is a song, sing it.

Life is a struggle, accept it.

Life is a tragedy, confront it.

Life is an adventure, dare it.

Life is luck, make it.

Life is life, fight for it."

He looked at the picture of the author and smiled. A small, wrinkled woman, a huge spirit from the Twentieth Century known as Mother Teresa.

Michael Rourke picked up his telephone and dialed an unlisted number as he glanced at his watch. It was two o'clock in the morning but the phone was answered before the third ring. "Sullivan..." a booming voice said with no hint of sleep.

"Morning Frank," Michael said. "I think it is time to begin... Can we meet?"

"Absolutely Sir, at the usual place and time this morning?"

"Yes, I think that would be appropriate."

"Certainly." There was a pause. "See you in three hours, Sir." The phone receiver slid quietly back into the cradle.

Michael looked at a printed note attached to a thick file that read, "Operation Phoenix." Below the title and in smaller type was a notation, "In Greek mythology the Phoenix was a long-lived bird, like an eagle only larger, that cyclically regenerated or was reborn. The Phoenix begins a new life after rising from the ashes of its predecessor." It was in fact the document that outlined his resignation and the plan to save the Rourke family and… hopefully the rest of humanity.

Chapter Sixty-Six

Thousands of miles away, just north of what at one time had been Spring-field, Missouri, time was also passing quickly. Already, the collapsed second entrance to the Fantastic Caverns had been opened. Materials were flowing routinely to what had been the intersection of Interstate 44 and Farm Road 123. From there AATVs hustled the materials to the Caverns.

To maintain security, a total of four of the counter-illuminated camouflage generators had been moved to cloak the landing zone, while eight maintained a cloaking screen over and around the towers. VTOL cargo planes managed to coordinate their flights between passes of satellites. Inflatable air bladders had been used to reposition many of the slabs of limestone that had fallen from the ceiling so long ago. Large pieces were shattered by focused sound waves and two or three of the AATVs, depending on the size of the pieces, were hooked up to them and drug out of the way.

Already, the entire upper cavern was strung with lights. Water pump stations and storage tanks had been installed. Dormitory spaces had been set up, food service kitchens were functional, even mechanical repair shops had been created... all in all, Chief Warrant Officer Wes Sanderson was "exceedingly well pleased" with the efforts of his men.

And Paul Rubenstein was now ready for Phase Two and make his run to the original Mount Yonah Retreat in northeast Georgia. He and his backup driver, Sergeant Haskins, along with their vehicle, trailer and a Harley Davidson motorcycle, were to be airlifted tomorrow. With any luck, they could have the items he had selected located, loaded and be ready to roll two days from now.

He was headed to grab a quick lunch at the "kitchen" when a shout stopped him. "Mr. Rubenstein, call Sir. Think it is your wife."

Paul jogged over to the communications desk. "This is Paul."

"Hello, husband, how are you?" Annie said.

"I am fine, wife. How are you?" Annie giggled.

"I am lonesome, with the kids gone and you gone… This house is awfully quiet," she said. "How is it all going?"

"Wes Sanderson's people have really done a great job, Annie," Paul said with enthusiasm. "You wouldn't recognize the place."

She laughed, "Probably not since I haven't seen it yet."

"Hey now," Paul said. "I sent you pictures."

"You did, but it is hard to judge things and get locations and stuff like that in my mind until I'm actually there… I miss you and I love you," she added in a soft tone.

Paul looked around, with no privacy; four communication technicians were watching and hanging on every word. *Crap*, he thought. Out loud he said, "I miss you too. I'm probably leaving tomorrow for the mountain. I'll give you a call tonight at the regular time, love you."

Paul blew a kiss into the phone and hung up. Then he turned to the communication technicians, "Hey guys, thanks for all the privacy," he smirked.

"Sure thing, Mr. Rubenstein. Any time," one of them said in a sing-song voice. Paul laughed with them and walked outside. Stopping to let his eyes adjust to the bright sunlight, he pushed his wire framed glasses back up on his nose. A wave of… something, washed over him. He looked across the camp, everything seemed normal. Most of the troopers worked at their chores still in uniform but several had stripped their uniform blouses and worked in sweat soaked t-shirts. He slowly turned to the left, his eyes searching but he wasn't sure for what.

He focused; silent thoughts began ricocheting around in his head. *On the far side of the gorge, was that a glint? Was it a reflection from a puddle of water?* He jerked the Browning High Power from his shoulder holster. *There, there that glint was again.* Paul dove hard to the left, hitting hard on his shoulder as a slug ripped through the spot in the time/space continuum where he had been just a microsecond ago.

Chapter Sixty-Seven

Paul rolled behind the nearest AATV, bringing his Browning to bear. "Across the gorge!" he yelled. "Shots came from across the gorge!" Return fire from Sanderson's troopers started chewing up the vegetation on that side of the gorge. Paul watched as one trooper armed with a rifle peeked around the corner of an AATV and snapped off a round at the shooter. Almost at the same instant, he was slammed back with a round to the chest.

Paul took off at a dead run for more cover. *Damnit, that's the last time I leave the Schmeisser by my bunk.* Rounding one of the water storage tanks he ran head long into one of Sanderson's troopers dragging a comrade. Noticing the blood soaked tunic of the downed man, he thought, *Doesn't look good. That's two down I can count.*

Pushing hard, he made a quick scan and ran to where three troopers were laying down a barrage of gunfire. "What's happened?" one shouted to Paul.

"Not sure," Paul said to one of the troopers. "Someone across the gorge by the cliff face, shooting at us."

One of the other troopers confirmed, "We started taking fire from just behind the cliff face on the other side of the ravine. Two of our men went down immediately, a third just got hit. Still no idea as to who is shooting at us or why."

There was a loud "whoosh" as a rocket powered grenade flew past their position and impacted the cliff face on the far side of the gully. The firing from across the gorge stopped. Paul thought either the shrapnel or the blast's concussion had nailed the shooter.

The trooper's gunfire slowed and then also stopped. Silence, silence you could almost taste fell across the area. Sanderson stood up, pointed to an NCO and gave orders to "Get a team over there and find out who the hell was shooting at us." Four troopers began a series of leap frog maneuvers; one moving, three covering.

It took several minutes after they vanished from sight for a radio to squawk next to Paul. "Chief, Haskins here. We have two bogies here, both down. You might want to come on over here and take a look."

"On my way, Haskins. Keep your eyes open." Chief Sanderson gave quick directions, several troopers moved off in different directions while Sanderson and two men moved off to see what Haskins had found. Paul stood up and followed them.

Chapter Sixty-Eight

Haskins keyed his radio. "Chief, Haskins. Where are you? Over."

"Right here, Haskins," Sanderson said, stepping out of the brush and dropping next to Haskins. Paul breathed slowly and deeply trying to catch his breath, noticing Haskins and his men were breathing almost normally. The troopers had assumed a security posture as Haskins was checking the bodies for any sign of life.

Haskins secured his radio. "One dead... one not. The young one, over there, is dead. This one," he pointed to the body closest to them. "He's alive but barely has a heartbeat. The kid was the shooter, this guy was his spotter. Kid had an old hunting rifle with a scope; I could only find a handgun on this one. Handgun plus this spotter scope."

Haskins looked at Paul. "Two questions Mr. Rubenstein. How did you spot him and how did he miss you? That is a shot of only about a hundred yards. No shot at all for an experienced shooter with a scope."

Paul shook his head. "Personally, I don't think he was that experienced. Answer to the first question, I felt him looking at me. Only way I can describe it. John Rourke told me a long time ago never to look at a man directly if you're going to take him out. 'He'll feel you watching him,' John said."

Haskins nodded. "That's true; never look directly at a man until you're ready to shoot."

Rubenstein nodded. "Answer to the second question is the same, I felt him looking at me and I moved a split second before he shot. A split second later... I'd be lying on that side of the gorge with a slug through my chest."

Sanderson turned to Haskins. "Move out and let's make sure these two aren't part of a larger team. Rubenstein and I will stay here until we get some help to take him across the gorge." Haskins nodded and gave a hand signal; an instant later he and the other three troopers had vanished into the brush. Sanderson keyed his mic. "I want three fire teams out: two down the slope of the gorge, the other one up and over the hill to link up with Haskins. Check the area for any stragglers.

"Throw me the rope," Sanderson said. "I want a pulley rigged up from that side of the gorge to this one. Let Doc know we have one who is tagged and bagged and one still alive. Rubenstein and I will send him over. Hurry up, throw us a line and we'll rig it on this side." Paul watched as three groups of men tore out of camp. He looked up just in time to see the coil of rope flying at him. He stepped aside and let it fall. "Paul, watch this guy, I'll rig the ropes.

Less than five minutes later the rope pulley was rigged and Sanderson had the unconscious man in a harness with a gag in his mouth, his hands and feet secured by flex-cuffs. Sanderson buckled the harness with a locking D-ring; he and Paul picked the man up and snapped the D-ring to the rope. Sanderson made a final check and jerked his fist up and down. "Move him out." A moment later the man was on solid ground with a Medic examining him.

The Medic signaled with a thumbs down gesture, the man had died. Sanderson took down the rope system, gave it a jerk and a man on the other side began rolling it up. "Come on Paul, hahaha," he said. "We gotta walk; no rides for us."

Paul followed Sanderson but failed to see the humor in the circumstances.

Chapter Sixty-Nine

"These cave walls won't fare well with gas powered exhaust fumes, we need to keep them at the front of the cave where we can keep the fumes pushed out." Richard Lee, the engineer, and Brandon Brice, the hydrogeologist, were briefing Sanderson and Rubenstein on their observations.

Brice was saying, "Water still flows through sinkholes and underground rivers below the main cave. Fantastic Caverns is a two level branch work cave. Both levels were, at one time, full of water but that was long ago. We will occupy the dry upper level. The lower level is a wet weather stream, carrying water during the rainy season through the cave to the discharge point outside the Caverns. We are going to make some modifications so that if we got a really big rain, we won't have water backing up from the lower level into the upper level, flooding it. Below the cave, all openings in the rock are water filled; that is below the water table. This water supplied wells in the area.

"What used to be called the Little Sac River still runs along the northeast side of the cave property, flowing through the deep valley. Long ago, the valley was not as deep, and the river level corresponded with the upper level of the cave. At that time the upper level of the cave was an active spring system, but as the river eroded deeper into the valley the water level in the cave lowered."

Richard Lee turned to Rubenstein and said, "Per your instructions, we are turning this cave into a multi-room, multi-level facility that will be extraordinary. We can house up to 1,000 people based on usable floor space in the main section; remember it is close to a half mile long. There will be a communications area, a clinic with a medical and dental operating theatre, a lab, a pharmacy, a cafeteria, an intensive care unit, meeting rooms, and more. While it is not really necessary under normal conditions, we are going to install an air filtration system and sewage plant. The air intake system is so intricate, it is meant to filter out radiation, that it will create a vacuum-like effect when you walk in. In the dormitory area, the sleeping quarters will be rows of metal bunk beds with wall lockers for personal clothing and other items.

"Maintenance won't be too difficult, but filters will have to be changed, machinery will have to be maintained, and food will have to be tracked, prepared and served. We are getting an inventory packed in right now that should last us about a year. In a few weeks we should have enough to last at least ten years.

"At each entrance, we will have a decontamination area; our ground based travels could put us into areas of residual high radiation. We'll have to plan on decontamination for both people and equipment; not to mention disposal methods for contaminated clothing and supplies. Besides the decontamination chamber, there will be three power plants with back up air and water purification equipment.

"We are inserting three 25,000-gallon water storage tanks and two 14,000-gallon diesel fuel storage tanks. Outside the cave we're putting in two 14,000 gallon underground fuel storage tanks, one for gasoline and another for diesel. That will give us fuel for the generators handling the electricity, sewage… everything really. The physical plant, concealed in the Caverns, will be divided into the following areas: dormitory space to house the population, the power section with generators for heating, electrical fuel and water supply tanks. Oh, and the armory…"

"How long before we have this area restored to the point all of it is disguised or camouflaged?" Rubenstein asked. "Won't do us any good to build this if anybody that walks by can see it."

"That's not a problem, the counter-illuminated camouflage generators will operate 24/7 until we have everything hidden. By the time a few weeks have passed, a casual observer won't notice anything. By the end of a couple of months… you would have to have pretty sophisticated detection gear to find anything."

"Surveillance and detection gear?"

"Yup, cameras, sensors… the whole nine yards and in three levels covering over two square miles and monitored from the communications area."

Sanderson quipped, "I think I may be a little claustrophobic being underground like this for long periods."

Rubenstein laughed. "We're going to take a lesson from the old Cold War fallout shelters. There will be a lot of digital LED clocks throughout the Retreat. That will help with our circadian rhythm and maintain sleep patterns. We are also installing 'windows'; these will be scenes of the outside world. John had something similar in the original Retreat. Gives you a sense of normal at least."

Lee nodded. "And the Communication Section will house everything from television and radio reception to computer modules that will have limited passive connection to the satellites we can tap into without risk of discovery. We will pump the television and radio feeds to each section of the cave for personal enjoyment and recreation. And we will have the ability to monitor all of the current U.S. military and news channels and those of the other countries that have been identified.

"Our transmittable communications will be limited to our own operations and will be encoded. The really long range stuff we will listen passively to. As soon as we start transmitting… we can be located. There will be two long range antennas that will be housed in piping underground. When, and if needed, these will be raised above the surface and activated."

"You're saying we can't transmit or we'll be located," Paul said. "We're transmitting now."

"Oh, my bad," Lee said. "I was talking about the emergency HAM radio system. That operates the way it always has. It can be tracked. Our encrypted communications can't be."

Rubenstein nodded. "Okay, you had me worried. This is a lot more complicated than the original Retreat John Rourke created."

Lee nodded. "Well Dr. Rourke was not looking at this many people, and he wasn't planning on interaction at any level with the rest of the world. He didn't figure there would be one."

Chapter Seventy

Sullivan spent the rest of the day gathering information and exhibits for that meeting. He and Zima poured over photos from all of the meetings the KI had participated in; none of their aircraft was an exact match to the ones Thorne had recorded and destroyed. Sullivan finally said, "Are we absolutely sure those birds belonged to the KI?"

Zima nodded. "Had to. They are the only other place with technology advanced so far above our own." Zima pondered the pictures and said, "General, I'm not a military guy so I may be way off base…"

"Go ahead. Spill it."

"Okay, these fighters look very much like the shuttle craft the KI have used since their first approach in our atmosphere. Very much but not identical. When the military develops a new weapon… how does that go? How do you keep it secret until it is fully tested?"

Sullivan frowned. "Well, Thorne told us that it wasn't much of a challenge to take those fighters out even when they had him outnumbered two to one. We know so damn little about the KI technology and out best source of information, The Keeper, hasn't been allowed much contact with us. It would sure be nice to have a chat with him and show him the pictures. We could get some real information instead of this damn speculation.

"One thing is for damn sure, Thorne was lucky they only came after him with two ships. We have to assume they either have more or they will in a matter of time. Problem is, we only have one ship like Thorne's. We know that the operational envelope of those KI fighters exceeds anything we have in our arsenal. One on one or one on a few, I think the combat training General Thorne is providing our pilots will make the difference."

Zima frowned. "But you're saying only if they were in a ship like Thorne's?"

Sullivan nodded, "Yeah Jose that is exactly what I'm saying. If we do find more ships like The Egg and we have pilots already trained to fly them… If the KI now had just those two ships and two pilots… how long before they have ten or twenty or more?" Sullivan began pacing then he walked to a globe on Zima's desk.

He picked it up and turned it over, almost in a whisper he mumbled, "Where the hell did those craft come from and how did those pilots train on them?" He studied the globe for almost two minutes, turning it from side to side.

"Jose, get your Astrophysicist down here, I've got some questions for him."

Chapter Seventy-One

Dr. Daniel Gregg came into Zima's office more than slightly out of breath. He pulled himself to attention in front of Sullivan. "General, I'm Dan Gregg, head of the Astrophysics Department."

Sullivan surveyed Gregg and smiled. "Dr. Gregg, I'd say you have put some time in uniform also. Am I correct?"

Gregg smiled and relaxed his posture. "Yes Sir, sorry Sir, force of habit around Generals. I was enlisted."

"Well right now I need your help Dr. Gregg, so let's take the rank off. I'm Frank Sullivan."

Gregg shook the outstretched hand. "Pleased to meet you Sir."

Sullivan frowned. "You're not gonna drop that Sir stuff, are you?"

Gregg shook his head. "No offense Sir, just doesn't seem right. Can't I just call you Sir?"

Sullivan laughed. "Then I'll just call you Doc. Doc, here's my problem. We have the KI stuck above Antarctica in a geo-synchronic orbit. Can you tell me how they would have developed new fighter craft, totally without our knowledge?"

"What is the altitude of their orbit, General?"

"Last time I looked it was 600 miles."

"What is the average altitude of our satellites and where are their sensors focused?"

"Hell if I know."

Gregg took a breath and walked to the white board on the wall and began drawing circles, each within each other. "Here's the deal, Sir, there are basically three types of Earth orbits. High Earth orbits are about 36,000 kilometers above the Earth. Medium Earth orbits are between 2,000 and 36,000 kilometers and the low Earth orbits between 180 and 2,000 kilometers. The KI are at 600 miles, which is 965 kilometers, or in the low Earth orbit.

"Now, high Earth orbits are usually for weather and some communications satellites. Satellites that are in medium Earth orbits include navigation and specialty satellites, designed to monitor a particular region. Most scientific satellites, including NASA's Earth Observing System fleet, have low Earth orbits.

"Remember also, most of our satellites today are truly ancient. Most from before The Night of the War. It has only been in the last few years that we have attempted any launches ourselves. Low Earth orbits start just above the top of the atmosphere, while high Earth orbits begin about one tenth of the way to the moon. Satellites closer to Earth are affected more by the pull of gravity, which is stronger. That means their orbits can decay and they crash back into the atmosphere.

"Now, I would have to research but off the top of my head I believe that in the orbital distance above 1,000 kilometers... well, to the best of my memory, none of them are positioned at or near the Antarctic full time. Virtually all of our satellites, except those the military have trained on the KI, are focused earthward. Your satellites are all below or right at the altitude of the KI, which means you can't see anything they are doing above or behind where your satellites can see."

Sullivan slammed his hand into the desk. "So, you are telling me the bastards took that position knowing we could not adequately watch their activities?"

Gregg scratched his head. "Well, yes Sir, isn't that what you would have done?"

Chapter Seventy-Two

Harmon Knowles, Director of the National Security Agency, frowned. "Mr. President, this seems… a little farfetched, if you ask me."

Michael Rourke nodded. "It does to me too, Director Knowles. However, circumstantially it seems to have some promise."

"Circumstantially?"

Michael nodded. "Yes Sir, first of all General Thorne finds an anomaly exactly where that anomaly was reported to be back in 1969. Second, he was attacked, without provocation, I might add, at those coordinates by vehicles we have identified as belonging to the KI.

"Third, that identification has been verified by reliable sources. Forth, we now have evidence that the specific area was in fact deeded to so-called Alien interests sometime before the Night of the War. Fifth, we know that my father and another man disappeared from the Mount Rushmore mission during an attack by craft belonging to the Aliens. And lastly, Mr. Knowles…" Michael steadied himself. "Lastly, Mr. Knowles, my father is still missing and your people haven't come up with a better explanation as to where he might be."

"Mr. President," Knowles began, "as you are aware, the entire Alaskan Peninsula is a disputed area between Russia and the United States. The U.S. claiming it because Alaska was our fiftieth state and the Russians claiming it as a possession since 1741 when Vitus Bering and Aleksei Chirikov landed on the Southeast coast line."

"Correct Mr. Knowles," Michael said. "However on March 30, 1867, Secretary of State William Seward agreed to a proposal from the Russian Minister in Washington, Edouard de Stoeckl, to purchase Alaska for $7.2 million."

"Unfortunately, Mr. President, while history bears that out, Russia disagrees and we have not been able to locate proof of that transaction following the Night of the War. I don't think it matters much since the entire area has been under glacial ice for half a century."

Michael smiled and opened his briefcase. "Here you go, Mr. Knowles. Hot off the press, so to speak, from the Hall of Records at Mount Rushmore."

He handed Knowles the purchase agreement and Bill of Sale signed just two years after the end of the American Civil War. "Now, Mr. Knowles, I expect you and the Secretary of State to present this proof to the Russians and ensure our sovereignty. We are mounting an expedition and I don't want any Russian interference. Do I make myself clear?"

Chapter Seventy-Three

Yonah in Georgia, back to the Caverns in Missouri. Paul figured it would take three, maybe four days, to get from Mount Yonah to the Caverns. That would be based on how quickly he found alternate routes between the two, so he had packed for a week. His main vehicle was a military truck with a double axle in back and all-wheel drive capability. Behind the double cab, which held a sleeping bunk, was a cargo area the size of an old Deuce and a Half. Behind it was a sixteen-foot, double axle trailer with five-foot sides, that would be filled to the brim.

He picked Haskins as his backup driver and outrider or scout. Once they arrived at the original Retreat, Haskins would rotate with Paul as driver, sleeping or scouting ahead on one of the Harley's stored at the Retreat. When the roads allowed, the Harley would be put on the trailer and hauled. When a different path needed to be found, Haskins would be the answer. Both the truck and the motorcycle would have GPS capabilities.

Because of the need for secrecy, the little convoy would only travel at certain times; times that no overhead satellites could detect them. Paul knew the biggest problem was there was no direct roadway across the Mississippi River between the states of Kentucky and Missouri. In fact the river lacked a single bridge crossing for a distance of over 300 miles from St. Louis to Memphis.

There were several locations where commercial ferries had operated before the Night of the War. A few still did, one was still called the Dorena-Hickman Ferry. It was 195 miles south of St. Louis and gave residents from the several small communities in Missouri a connection to the town of Hickman, Kentucky, on the opposite bank. Folks from larger towns in the area also benefited from the ferry.

Paul told Haskins, "It will be a significant time saver for us if everything goes well. We need to determine if the ferry is still operational, and if the river or the weather might have other ideas. If the water levels are too high or it's too windy, we're going to have to wait; that thought doesn't thrill me much. We could be stuck there for a few hours or a few days."

Paul's maps showed that on the Kentucky side, the dock was located just off of Kentucky Route 94 on the western side of Hickman. The latitude/longitude coordinates for GPS were 36.567744° N, 89.212022°W. If they made it across to the Missouri side, they would leave the river where Missouri Highway A hits it.

*****

Part of the plan that Paul Rubenstein was implementing relied on three people to maintain secrecy. One was the influence that Michael Rourke, still President of the United States, continued to have. The second was the influence that General Frank Sullivan, Air Force Chief of Staff, had. The third was a person Paul had never and would never meet; an Air Force Intelligence Technician, Staff Sergeant named James Lancon. Lancon's grandfather had served with Sullivan years ago and they remained friends.

Lancon's mission was simple; he erased the tracking information associated with any GPS monitor assigned to the Dog Soldiers, Wes Sanderson's Spec Ops Marines, the President himself and seven that had been surreptitiously assigned to each member of the Rourke family. Including the one that Paul Rubenstein carried on this mission. The likelihood of GPS activity on the mainland ever creating a question was remote; however, now it was virtually impossible as long as Lancon did his part.

As John Rourke would say, "It pays to plan ahead."

Chapter Seventy-Four

For two hours they had travelled in a steady downpour. On the motorcycle, Haskins' boots and blue jean pants were soaked through. His rain jacket and rain pants had tried to do their job, but the rain had won. He was cold, wet and tired. So tired, he didn't notice at first that the rain was slowing down. An hour later, the pavement was dry and the sky was clear as he pulled to the side of the road and stopped.

He flicked the kick stand out and stepped off the Harley. Stripping his helmet and gloves, he unsnapped the rain jacket and took it off. Opening the cuffs of the rain pants and balancing with one hand against the bike, he pulled first one leg and then the other over his riding boots and waited until Paul pulled the truck and trailer off behind him. "Weather sure looks better," Paul said.

"I'll say," Haskins replied as he shook the rain suit as dry as he could then rolled them into a single bundle and put them in one of his saddle bags. "I don't know about you but I'm drenched. How about an early camp this evening?"

Paul nodded. "Sounds good to me." Glancing at his watch as he pushed his wire framed glasses back up on his nose, he replied, "There is a scenic overlook about half way up this mountain; let's push on to that, probably another fifteen or twenty minutes. Plenty of room for both the bike and truck and trailer."

"I appreciate it; I'm soaked to my underwear."

Half way up the side of the mountain gave them a panoramic view of the valley. What had once been a scenic overview was reduced to simply a wide shelf that provided little except a flat area to pitch the tent. Looking around Paul said, "Looks like the sky is clear as far as I can see, I think we either outran the rain or it took a turn."

Haskins nodded as he broke out a bundle of paracord from his saddle bag. "At least we will be able to dry out. I'll string this up between those two trees by the drop off over there. With the sun and this breeze, our clothes and gear should be dry in an hour or so."

"You get that and I'll pitch the tent," Paul said, walking to the back of the cargo truck and pulling out the tent. Looking around he picked a spot and in just minutes had the ground cloth spread and dome tent staked down over it. "Now let's get the flexible poles laid out," he said to himself and pulled out bundles of aluminum sections connected with elastic cord. He had used composite flexible poles for years when he took the kids and Annie camping but had one break on him a while back.

Even though it had been made of carbon fiber, it had its limits. While it could be bent drastically and would return to its normal shape, the problem is they can break. Once, he had messed up the threads connecting a pole and tried to force it. When it broke, some of those carbon fibers flew into his hand, leaving the remaining broken end very sharp. He had taken a ball point pen apart and used one section to slide the broken ends in and duct taped the whole thing, saving the camping trip. He had gotten most of the carbon fibers out of his hand but the couple he couldn't see created an infection that required a visit to the ER a few days after the trip.

Rather than replace the broken one, he had gone to all metal and never had the problem again. He just had to be careful where he stepped as he laid out the poles. While they would not break, they would bend and could retain a bend caused by a misstep.

By the time he had the tent up, he heard Haskins whistling. Paul turned and broke out in laughter. With the exception of his boots, a rifle and pistol belt, Haskins was naked as a "Jay bird."

"Okay, bring 'em over boss. We may have to get out some long johns though; it is already getting a little chilly."

Paul waved and started collecting firewood. Haskins set to building a fire ring out of fist sized rocks that had rolled down from above their location. Remembering John Rourke's admonishment to 'plan ahead,' he dug out a change of clothes and then he stripped down and hung his damp garments. "Put some clothes on Haskins."

"You got modesty issues?"

193

Paul laughed. "If I did I lost them right after The Night of the War when John Rourke and I were walking naked through Albuquerque because our clothes had radiation on them. Your shiny, skinny white butt will reflect light. I don't want to have to evacuate this camp site tonight at a full run with a naked guy running behind me, showing where we are."

Thirty minutes later they had moved the vehicle closer to the campsite and had a cook fire going. An hour later, they had finished the freeze dried stew, cleaned the pot and plates and were relaxing, leaning back against a fallen tree with their rifles propped next to them. Haskins glanced at his watch, stood up and said, "I'm going to check our clothes. They should be dry by now." He walked over to the clothes, touched several to make sure they were dry and started pulling them down from the line. Moving back toward Paul he suddenly stopped, standing stock still.

Haskins shifted the clothes to his left hand and with his right, grabbed the pistol grip of his CAR 15. He hissed a low "psssst" to catch Paul's attention.

Paul took a look back at Haskins, frowned and then understood and rolled to his left. He could see movement up the hill side and down the road they had not traveled yet. He gripped his Browning High Power in his right hand.

Haskins worked the action handle on his CAR 15, pulling a round from the top of the 30-round magazine and sliding it into the chamber. Jogging quickly back to the log they had been leaning against, he hopped over the log and sat down, dropped the clothes and brought the rifle up to the ready position.

He had taken a position to Paul's right and his eyes swept down the hill and back along the path they had driven. Both men listened, senses on alert.

Paul pulled the Schmeisser to him and slowly, quietly, jacked a 9mm round into the chamber.

"Hello the camp," a hidden voice called out from the brush.

"Can we help you?" Paul shouted.

"Yeah, lay down your guns and let's talk."

Haskins hollered, "How about we keep our guns and talk? What do you want?"

"Hee, hee, hee. We want what you got. Give us the keys to the motorcycle and the truck, add your guns to ours and we'll leave you alone. You boys can walk back down the hill. We won't bother you none."

Haskins turned to Paul and whispered, "Whatcha think Boss? Could be just the one…"

Paul shook his head. "Not likely. Stay ready, I don't think this is going to end well." Then he looked up and shouted, "Don't think that is going to happen! You could just back out of here and we could avoid the bloodshed."

A shot rang out and the slug drilled into the log Paul and Haskins were behind. Another rang out from a different direction. "At least two bad guys. Can you see them?" Paul whispered.

"No."

"You hold your fire until you can, let them think they got you. I'm going to move over by that big rock. When you have a shot, take it." Paul was up and running, firing the Schmeisser on full auto with one hand to cover his movement. He dove, sliding in the dirt as another round ricocheted off the boulder he was now behind.

"Damn it," a voice rang out from up the hill. "I'm hit. He's got a machine gun."

"Shut up and get ready to move," a voice, obviously the leader, shouted. "There's four of us and only two of them, we got 'em out numbered."

Paul smiled and thought, *Thanks for the information Pal. Four mountain Red Necks against us is not enough.* He looked over at Haskins; he held the rifle ready, aiming under the log. Paul held up four fingers then gave the "okay" sign. Haskins nodded, he was ready. Paul shouted, "Okay, okay. You hit my friend, he's hurt… maybe dead! I give up!"

The voice came back to him, "Stand up, hands in the air, gun on the ground."

"Can't," Paul yelled back. "I think I broke my ankle sliding behind this rock. I'll lay the gun on the rock, stand up and when I'm braced against the boulder I'll raise my hands. Okay?"

"Throw the machine gun out first. Do it!"

Paul pitched the Schmeisser in front of the boulder and using the boulder pulled himself upright, favoring his right leg. The Browning was stuck in his belt behind him. Paul was finally erect with his hands over his head. "Okay, stand there just like that. Bill, Joe... check the other one. Frank, come on down with me."

As soon as they broke cover, Paul smiled. One of them had a bullet crease from Paul's Schmeisser along the side of his head. He had slung his rifle, a lever action, probably a .30-30, over one shoulder and was tying a bandana over the wound as he walked down. *Amateur,* Paul thought. The two approaching Haskins were no better. They carried bolt action hunting rifles, but one had his rifle cocked back over one shoulder and the other had slung his and pulled a big bowie knife.

"Ain't no sense in wasting ammo," he said with a smile that showed a ragged, almost toothless grin. The leader maintained a little weapons discipline. He carried his scoped, bolt action rifle waist high and loosely pointed toward Paul... that is until his lead foot slid to one side on the leaves and loose rocks of the hillside.

Paul moved, jerking the Browning from the small of his back and fired a double tap as soon as the barrel came on line with the target. Haskins opened up on the two men approaching him with a series of rapid fire single shots.

Paul caught the leader high in the shoulder with one round; the other missed meat but knocked the rifle from his hand. The man staggered and fell back. Paul shifted to the man with the bullet crease. He was fumbling, trying to unsling his bolt action rifle as Paul squeezed off three rounds and dove for the Schmeisser.

Haskins had risen to a kneeling position behind the log, firing quick, well-aimed shots at his aggressors. Of the two gunmen coming at him, one was down and still. The other was behind a tree screaming obscenities and working the bolt on his rifle, and firing as blood soaked the left shoulder of his filthy shirt.

Paul spun in his direction cutting loose with a string of 9mm shredders from the Schmeisser, dropping the man. He felt and heard a round zing past his head and turned back to see the leader on the ground. His rifle lay to one side with a shattered stock and he had a heavy revolver pointed at Paul.

The man started to shout something but that was when Haskins put a round in the man's opened mouth. Blood and bone blasted out the back of the man's head in a pink spray, clots of brains completed the mix.

Chapter Seventy-Five

Sullivan sat in the Operations Center; communications from each individual element of Operation Hay Stack were linked. Those assets that had the greatest distance to travel had launched days before in order to be on station for Zero Hour. It was approaching quickly.

The Naval Chief of Staff sat to Sullivan's right side at the big table, the Chief of Staff for the Marines to his right. To Sullivan's left, the Army Chief of Staff was speaking with the coordination center for West Coast Operations. Directly in front of Sullivan were three lights: one green for "Launch the Operation," one red for "Stop the Operation," one black for "Delay the Operation." He looked at the two clocks on the console. The one on the left was counting down to Zero Hour, only three minutes remained. The clock on the right was frozen, both hands at twelve o'clock. It would track the length of the operation.

On the wall there was a large computer screen; blinking lights showed the position of all stationary assets. There was no indicator where The Egg and the air mission's planes were. Sullivan hoped what he was looking at was exactly what the Russians and the KI were seeing. Nothing but a monitoring mission in the North Pacific, taking readings from the Ring of Fire volcanic system.

This system had grown in importance ever since sub-oceanic cracks in the Earth's crust threatened the safety of the free world. Luckily John Thomas Rourke had led a successful attempt at sealing those cracks. Had he not been able to steal from a mad man, Deitrich Zimmer and his Nazi storm troopers, the world may have truly perished. Monitoring missions were now about as common place as weather balloons had been before The Night of the War. In front of Sullivan, the left clock kept ticking off seconds.

Chapter Seventy-Six

Onboard The Egg, Thorne was monitoring the hologram screen. He was particularly interested in the cloaking screen that hid the four VTOL cargo planes beneath him. It was essential that none of the planes strayed beyond the umbrella of cloaking technology, keeping them invisible. One momentary slip would be enough to blow the element of surprise completely out of the water.

Thorne only had one fear as he stewarded his charges northeast across the glacial expanse of what at one time had been Canada. Would the Alien known as The Creator have some way of detecting his craft that none of them knew anything about? Some type of Alien "transponder" their instruments could not detect? There was still much to know and much to learn about The Egg.

Next to him, Akiro Kuriname sat quietly observing the hologram. He had taken quickly to the flight deck of The Egg. Muscle memories of his time sitting where Thorne sat had returned at an incredible rate. Incredible, particularly since prior to the sessions with Blackman and The Keeper, he had no memory at all of piloting a craft like this. Like Thorne, he wore a flight suit with a pistol belt on his side. Unlike Thorne, there was a harness that held his beloved "Saiai no hōmotsu," his "Beloved Treasure," his Samurai sword, on his back.

Thorne glanced to the side. "How are you doing, Akiro?"

"I am fine, I am hopeful that we will be able to locate my friend and return him to his family. I am also hopeful that we may find and retrieve the others being held at the pyramid and..." He smiled. "And liberate sufficient craft such as this one to protect our world and put a stop to this madness. I am hopeful for all of these things."

"I noticed you and General Sullivan talking privately before we launched. Care to share, anything I need to know about?"

Akiro shook his head. "Not really, he asked that I pay special attention to the VTOL below us on the far left."

"Eagle One?"

Kuriname nodded.

"May I ask why… I mean, why that one?" Thorne asked, curiously.

"Certainly, because that one is the plane carrying the President, Michael Rourke."

Thorne jerked back to face Kuriname. "What, what the hell… What the hell is he doing on an operation like this? What the hell is Sullivan thinking allowing it in the first place?"

Kuriname smiled a sedate smile. "General Thorne, I take it you do not have much experience with the members of the Rourke inner circle. Let me put your mind to rest. General Sullivan knew better than to engage in a battle he could not win. Michael Rourke is on a mission to find his father, my friend, John Rourke. So am I. There is no amount of pressure or protocol that could have kept Michael Rourke off this mission. My only concern is if something happens to John Rourke, to say someone will suffer horrific consequences would be… simply a gross understatement."

"Can I ask you another question?" Thorne said.

"Certainly."

Thorne cleared his throat. "Okay, I mean no disrespect but do you really know how to use that chopper you have on your back?"

In less than the blink of an eye, Kuriname had drawn the sword and placed the edge on Thorne's Adam's apple… without drawing a drop of blood. Thorne said nothing; he had not seen Kuriname move and had not known he had moved until he felt the blade. "Yeah, okay… you do."

Thorne keyed his microphone, "Eagle Brood, this is Momma Bird, do you have your individual targets identified and keyed in?"

Each VTOL pilot gave his or her call sign and an "Affirmative."

"Roger that," Thorne said. "We are over the target and I am cutting the cloak in three, two, one… NOW! Good luck!" He dove behind Eagle One and landed just long enough to discharge his passenger before leaping back into the sky for fly cover. As he ascended, he said, God speed.

Halfway across the Pacific, the Operations Center went silent as four blips appeared above the Denali location. Operation Hay Stack was on, it had launched. Sullivan noticed it was strangely quiet. None of the surface ships were transmitting; neither were the submarines. He looked up at a technician. "We still have communications?"

The technician checked all of the leads. "Yes Sir, just nothing coming in."

Then all hell broke loose.

Chapter Seventy-Seven

Eagles One and Two landed near to their assigned entry point and disembarked personnel. Michael Rourke, dressed in black jeans and shirt covered in Arctic extreme cold weather gear, led his Posse. The device he held in one hand detected the counter-illuminated camouflage technology as expected. Walking straight ahead, he passed through the cloak and disappeared into the tunnel on the other side. The rest of the teams followed.

The tunnel mouth itself was almost forty feet across and half that distance tall. It came out of a cliff face with an overhang that prevented it from being seen from above. The lay of the land had made it difficult to observe the tunnel mouth from ground level. Michael wondered for exactly how long. The tunnel mouth for the first fifty feet was weathered, looking more like the mouth of a cave rather than a tunnel.

Fleming, one of Michael's Posse said, "I would guess between the legends surrounding evil spirits and the harsh terrain, folks didn't do much exploring around here."

"Probably, that and the camouflage technology," Michael said. "But remember there are reports of folks disappearing in this region. Maybe they found the tunnels, and then were found themselves and taken prisoner."

Akiro Kuriname stopped sixty feet inside the tunnel and began removing his Arctic gear, the rest followed suit. Freed from the bulky pants and parka, Michael pushed down on his pistol belt and adjusted the Pachmayr gripped butt of the Stalker, his Magnum Sales converted Ruger Super Blackhawk .44 Magnum single action with a 2X Leupold scope hanging on his left hip. On his right hip he wore the handmade copy of Jack Crain's Life Support 1. An original Smith and Wesson Model 29 .44 Magnum rode in an Alessi shoulder rig under his left arm. In his right hand was the CAR 15 with a 30-round magazine. He slipped the musette bag with extra magazines over his head in a cross body carry.

By the time he was finished, the rest of the squads had done likewise and were ready to move out. Fleming said, "I don't like this, it is like we're walking down a street. There's no cover or concealment if we get attacked."

"No choice," Michael said. "No other way to access the pyramid. Let's go." He adjusted the headband straps on the night goggles and turned them on. The world went green.

*****

Eagles Three and Four teams also had left a pile of Arctic gear in the tunnel before proceeding. Eagle Three's team leader, Dog Soldier Benjamin Nehen, was large for a Native American, dark skinned with high cheek bones and jet black hair cut in a short buzz. "I don't like this," he said to Darrel Avonaco, Eagle Four's leader as they moved silently down the tunnel viewing their progress through the two-dimensional green world of NVGs.

"I don't either. There is nothing to get behind for cover if we have to fight."

Charlie Blackhorse, walking just behind Avonaco piped up, "Then let's just not have to fight."

Chapter Seventy-Eight

Half a world away at the John Thomas Rourke Survival Academy's Camp Zero, the Rourke and Rubenstein children were trying to deal with the supposed accidental death of one of their class instructors. Nothing was making sense; and it was about to get much worse.

"This still doesn't explain the things that have been happening here," Natalie said, persistent. "Madison's death? Paula says there's no way she could have died from that fall. And what about all the other things that have been happening?"

"That's enough." Sandy Tempest, the instructor they called Ma, raised her hands, her sharp tone returning with a vengeance. "In all my time as an instructor here, we've never had to deal with a situation like this. I'm going to call Mr. Dickson and recommend that we cancel the course. As soon as we round up our strays, you're all going home."

The harsh announcement hit John Michael like a slap. Ma's reaction was completely unfair. It wasn't his fault that Alma and Kevin had lied about who they were, wasn't his fault that Tim and Paula had snuck off. If the adults had just had been truthful, none of this would have happened. There was no reason to punish everyone.

Ma appeared ready to make good on her threat. She unclipped a walkie-talkie from her belt, but as she raised it there was a flash of movement from somewhere off to John's right, and then Ma staggered back.

John's brain struggled to process what he had just seen. A tree limb seemed to have sprouted from Ma's chest… No, it was a crude spear. But why was it—? A scream went up and then the camp erupted into chaos. The other students scattered, crashing into one another in full panic mode.

*****

Natalia looked up when the knock sounded on the door to the Presidential Residence Wing. She thought, *A report already? Can't be… it's too soon unless there has already been trouble.* She opened the door and saw Tim Shaw. "Sorry to bother you Natalia but there may be a problem."

"Is Michael alright?" Concern leapt to her face.

"It is not him and I'm not sure there is even is a problem but…"

Natalia grabbed the sleeve of Shaw's jacket. "What is it, Tim?"

Shaw tried to smile but the effort didn't work, "Probably nothing… but we have lost contact with the Survival Academy. May just be something electrical but they aren't answering the phone or the radio. I'm sure it's nothing and they will have it fixed shortly."

Epilogue

Why…do…your…people…come? The creature known as The Creator asked.

John Rourke examined the view screens watching the progress of the teams as they moved down the twin tunnels. He thought, *They have no cover at all, if the Aliens attack they don't have a chance.* Then he saw two familiar figures, one dressed in black carrying a CAR 15 and wearing two large single action revolvers—Michael. The other also dressed in black but with a sword strung across his back—Akiro Kuriname.

Rourke turned from the view screens. "They have come for me… not for you. You must not attack them, they won't stand a chance."

They… carry… weapons… they… are… armed.

"Yes, they are; they do not understand," Rourke said, pleading. "Let me talk to them, I can make them understand."

They… are… armed.

Rourke knew an armed attack would never work, he had to stop Michael and the others before The Creator did. "Please, let me speak to them. This is wrong; their deaths are not necessary." He thought desperately. "It would not be correct, it would not be accurate!"

The creature stood impassive, the only movement was the head which periodically moved from side to side; on a human it could have been interpreted as quizzical or thoughtful. Correct… accurate… must… be… correct… must… be… accurate.

Then Rourke felt something, a "gentle probe" in his mind. He looked at the creature but the probe was not coming from it. Barely a whisper at first, less than an impression, more like a mental breeze, a thought began to form in John's mind. *Yes John, it is me…*

*****

Paula Rourke found no refuge in the darkness of night. They—she, and the other 'Rourke' children—could not remain at Camp Zero, that would be a death sentence; one that came with a guarantee. *I have to find the others,* she thought. *We have to figure out who we can trust.* With a start, she suddenly realized, *We can't trust anyone but ourselves. Why were we attacked? Who attacked us? Without knowing who and what had motivated the attack, it is impossible to determine the safest course. Assume the worst,* she thought. *Until we know differently, assume that we are being hunted and plan ahead.*

*****

"Soon," The Captain said, aloud. "Soon the forces of the KI shall regain their rightful place as the rulers of this world. Soon we will have sufficient trained combat pilots to put down the resistance of any of the countries on the planet."

The Russian Colonel, Mikhail Sergeyevich, smiled. "And soon my people will join you in this historic plan. Our peoples joined in friendship for all times." Inwardly the Colonel smiled and thought, *At least long enough for us to master your technology then we shall make slaves of you as well.*

"Yes my friend," the Captain said, smiling. "With your assistance and training, you are helping my people improve their combat skills to the point our two forces will be unstoppable." *At least,* he thought, *until such time as we no longer require your assistance then you also shall fall under our domination.*

Sergeyevich raised his glass in a toast. "Long, long ago our illustrious leader, Vladimir Karamatsov, set in motion World War III. Mother Russia was to rise as the leader of the new world. But for Rourke." He spit the name out. "Now all of these years later, generations have come and gone and now our vengeance is about to descend on John Thomas Rourke and his hellish family. If only Karamatsov could be here to see it. His death will finally be avenged."

The Captain returned the toast. "You knew this Karamatsov?"

"Oh, yes. I knew him well."

The Captain looked puzzled. "But how is that so?"

207

Sergeyevich smiled. "Oh, my Captain, that is very simple. The Rourkes were not the only ones to survive the death of that world."

CAMP ZERO series is based on characters created by
Jerry Ahern, Sharon Ahern and Bob Anderson in The Survivalist series.

For more information
visit: www.speakingvolumes.us

Surgical Strike series

For more information
visit: www.speakingvolumes.us

The Defender series

For more information
visit: www.speakingvolumes.us

They Call Me the Mercenary series
Axel Kilgore (Jerry Ahern)

For more information
visit: www.speakingvolumes.us

The Takers series

For more information
visit: www.speakingvolumes.us

TAC Leader series

For more information
visit: www.speakingvolumes.us

www.ingramcontent.com/pod-product-compliance
Lightning Source LLC
Chambersburg PA
CBHW032045240626
47154CB00003B/1077